What You Are

STORIES

M.G. VASSANJI

DOUBLEDAY CANADA

Library and Archives Canada Cataloguing in Publication

Title: What you are / M.G. Vassanji.
Names: Vassanji, M.G., author.
Description: Short stories.
Identifiers: Canadiana (print) 20210113723 | Canadiana (ebook) 20210113758 | ISBN 9780385692885 (hardcover) | ISBN 9780385692892 (EPUB)
Classification: LCC PS8593.A87 W53 2021 | DDC C813/.54—dc23

Cover design: Lisa Jager
Cover image: Bahador/Unsplash

Printed and bound in Canada

Published in Canada by Doubleday Canada,
a division of Penguin Random House Canada Limited

www.penguinrandomhouse.ca

10 9 8 7 6 5 4 3 2 1

Penguin Random House
DOUBLEDAY CANADA

To the elderly men and women
confined to care homes
victims of the Virus. 2020

CONTENTS

THE SEND-OFF

In the evenings after dinner the five of us would gather around her in the living room. We were Firoz, the eldest, my sisters Naila and Safia, myself, and Salim, the youngest. Mother would be sitting on her large bed, both legs pulled up, one crossed and the other stretched out in front, cutting patterns from a bolt or two for the next day's sewing, or catching up on her bookkeeping. The large six-band radio atop our display cabinet was the other focal point of the room, playing Hindi or English songs, and bringing us news from the BBC, which also told us the exact time, "eighteen hours Greenwich Mean Time," by which to set our clock for nine p.m. Dar es Salaam. All the day's news we would discuss then and enthusiastically greet the songs as they were announced, especially those of Elvis or Connie Francis or Cliff Richard. Our best evenings were when Mother or Naila told a story, Mother from her younger days, Naila something she'd brought back from school.

Now in another world a continent and an ocean away we had gathered by her bed once more, this time to help release her from her life—as the righteous euphemism puts it—but in fact to watch her finally die. To watch and cheer, I couldn't help thinking. It's all over and done, the burden has lifted from our lives. The solemnity at the nursing home felt as false as a badly acted drama. This was celebration.

The doctor was reached on the phone and said to increase the morphine. The duty nurse looked at me, I turned to my cousin, a former nurse. Maimuna nodded, "It will make it easier for her." I said, "Yes, okay." The syringe went in.

It had fallen upon me to decide whether or not to give her a chance to revive; two years ago I had said let's wait, everyone agreed, and she revived. And told more stories. But this time a sense of finality had come over us, the hovering angel of death had been allowed to descend. People justify with all sorts of reasons end-scenes such as this; ours was: old age, it's time. Leading busy lives, we had little time for her and had grown weary of waiting. And it was quite apparent that the home needed another bed.

I don't want to wallow in guilt, nor do I wish to excuse myself. I've learned irony and I wish simply to record the death of my mother. And to remember her a little, allow that other world to tug at me before it's completely vanished.

I went to stand at the door, before me this scene at her bedside, behind me the long empty corridor bright with a fluorescent sunshine reflected cheerlessly off the yellow walls. My two sisters were beside the bed on one side, my cousin and my wife Jena on the other, and at the foot sat Mariam, the woman who came to help her for one hour every day. She would not have missed this finale. She had earned it. My two brothers, both out of town, had yet to arrive.

Mother's face looked surprisingly radiant, as she lay under a blanket breathing in shallow rapid gurgles, the air making its tortured way through her congested trachea. An oxygen tube ran under her nose. She had been returned from hospital at my say-so and upon the ER resident's recommendation. Was it worth, after a few hours of lying on a gurney in a hospital corridor, putting her through the extra ordeal of an insertion up her nose to clear her breathing passages? "We'll take her back, then," I pronounced, after a moment's hesitation, feeling only slightly coerced with a tightness in the stomach. The resident, a young woman, had looked relieved. It was two in the morning, and more stretchers had queued up in the corridor.

Her breathing became lighter, and the four women in the room, at Mariam's practiced instigation ("She's ready to go"), began chanting fervently all together—*Allahuma salli ala . . .*—their faces pinched, their eyes lowered, swaying backward and forward. The room filled up with the chorus. God bless the Prophet, indeed, but my mother was having none of this. She was a stubborn woman. Her face, still radiant at her age, was composed, her lips were just open, and I swear I saw the familiar grim smile on her face, and I imagined her saying, I'm not going yet, you pray as much as you like. That voice. They gave up after a while and sat back cheerfully to chat. False alarm. I returned to sit down with them at the bedside.

In lowered voices we told stories about her, marvelled at her eventful life and resilience, her funny ways in the last couple of years; and we recalled stories about each other when we were young. This dying moment had brought us closer, we who had lived eight people to two rooms as children, but recently had so little time to see each other. She had gathered us, as we gathered around her when we were children.

That scene of my mother's last hours in the nursing home lingers: the change in breathing, the frantic piety of the cheerleading, her refusal to go, and the resumption of chatter. This rigmarole was repeated three times, and each rehearsal it brought an irreverent smile to my face. Perhaps I was a bit hysterical in the circumstances and simply wished to laugh out my tension. What were the prayers for? I suppose—no longer believing in them—they were to ease the soul's passage out; but it seemed more a way of pushing it through in a collective heave-ho: There you go, Mummy, no point sticking around; it's going to happen, let it happen. Go.

We've become a practical lot in Canada. We like to do things with maximum efficiency and little fuss.

The gentle lines on her old-pretty face bore all the versions of her that I could recall over the years, one image impressed upon another. And as I watched her, the frantic prayers failing to coax her into leaving, I couldn't help thinking, You show them Mummy! You'll go when you are ready. Give me some time.

In the Indian tradition, sons look after their parents when they get old. They are also favoured. I, the second-youngest, was her favourite, her *laal.* So she would say to me. So I believed. She became a widow at thirty-three when my father died of a sudden heart attack. She never remarried; to do so—and she had good offers, I know now—would have been to abandon her children to adoption. Others drowned unwanted infant girls in milk, our widows were asked to give up their children in order to remarry. She liked to tell the story of Shravan, the young man who would carry both his old parents on his shoulders to take them for their pilgrimages; one day in a forest he put them down to rest under a tree by a river, and as he stepped to the water and bent down to take a sip, a king who was out on a hunt mistook him for a deer and shot him with an arrow. I was never quite certain what the lesson was, but evidently Shravan was a devoted son, just as she was the devoted mother who had foregone a secure life with companionship for our sakes. When the great Indian epic *Mother India* came to town, she sent us all to watch it. She herself, minding her store, must have been the only Asian woman who never saw it. The story was about a widow who, despite her travails, and the harassment of lecherous men, brought up her boys as responsible, upright citizens in the new India.

One evening when we were all gathered in the sitting room, she as usual on her bed with scissors and cloth, the radio playing song requests, she said to me, "No, Karim, you won't look after me when you're grown up, you'll just throw me aside." I must have boasted of my undying devotion to her and therefore protested with all my ten-year-old's indignation, "Of course I will! I will always look after you, Mummy!" To prove which I wrote down a note promising precisely that: When I grow up I will always look after Mummy. And I signed it, and she put it in her bosom with a smile. My promissory note, my *hundi*. But at twenty I went to America to study and we never lived together again. I wonder why she let me go, using all her savings for the plane ticket; and I wonder where my note ended up. It was never mentioned again in my presence, perhaps out of kindness to me.

In Toronto, no matter who else had visited her, if her *laal* had not arrived yet, she would observe, simply, "No one came, today." And when I walked in, she'd announce, "Look, Karim has arrived." To any nurse who happened to be around, she would proudly point at me: "My son." Inevitably my wife Jena, if she was with me, would complain afterwards, "You see! She didn't even notice me," and with sinking heart—for I had hoped she hadn't noticed—I would explain, "She is old." I have often wondered, Why do we take abuse from our children yet not tolerate an aged parent's slightest oversights?

She had been practically bundled off to the nursing home by Naila and Firoz. One Sunday I saw her in her apartment, frail but on her feet, and she made me tea. The following week she was in a wheelchair by her bed in the home, looking dazed in an alien world, her lips compressed. She didn't speak a word. This was not what she had consented to. Later, often, she'd pronounce, "It's a prison." A *qaid-khano*. She who had always been independent, negotiating a man's world. And so it was hardly surprising to come upon her once in a while saying, "Send me back to Dar es Salaam, I can look after myself." She would have stayed up half the night nursing this resolve and making her plans. We would laugh and cajole, "Mummy, you can't even get up from your wheelchair!"

"I can."

It was not a bad place, the home; it was clean, and the dining room was small and not crowded; the corridors were not crammed with old folks drooling or crying, as in the other places we had seen. But which nurse attended her on any given day was the luck of the draw; there were some who were kind and called her mother, and others who could easily have stood guard at a concentration camp. The home was there to break you if you had not already given up the will to live. When I saw Mother being heaved by two strong nurses into the cradle of a machine to be lifted like a sack, I wanted to run down the corridor and scream. Nobody deserved this. I was never around again to witness this sight.

—

We can recall hardships, existence at disaster's edge when every penny counted, moments when the elder siblings fought so viciously that Mother, in desperation, threatened to walk away to the sea, less than a mile away, and drown herself. No, Mummy, please! We'll be good! Don't go. Moments when she simply sat down and beat her chest raw and wept. Yet none of us would now say our life was unhappy. We fondly recall the best parts, are aware of the bonds we formed, and would rather not pause to examine the scars. We had been sent to school and in the end survived and thrived. She on the other hand ailed and decayed, became gradually alone and unhappy, unwanted—and was finally relegated to the nursing home to break and die.

I recall her sitting on her high stool behind the counter of her corner shop, looking over the two doorways, brooding, picking her chin. After many experiments she ended up specializing in children's clothes; the customers were our African neighbours. Except for a few days at every month's end, and during the month of Ramadan, business was slow. Over the fifteen years she ran the shop, she spent all her capital, which was the small insurance benefit she had received after my father's death, but we all completed high school. Two of us went to university. Mother herself had quit school after grade six, because, as she told the story many times, her father withdrew her, saying, What's the use of so much learning? She had cried. She could have been a teacher, like the ones I had in my early years, who had barely two years more of schooling than she.

There are things about our parents' lives that we are not equipped to notice until we ourselves grow up and they hit us, stark epiphanies. Then we see the darker side of the world we came from. Of the few hundred shops run by Asians in our town, hers was the only one run by a woman. A young, pretty widow with small children and little money. Years later when she let slip a remark, I realized the obvious, that it was a man's world she had negotiated through, facing the sly comment, the lascivious look, the obscene suggestion when she was late in her instalments to the collectors who came by every so often. She always took me or my younger brother with her when she went to purchase from the wholesalers, and later when we were barely in our teens she sent the two of us on our own to deal with the men. She faced the humiliation of having to ask the tailor next door to mind her shop so she could go upstairs to our flat to use the toilet, the rest of us being in school. Early every morning she cooked our dinner, and sent us off to school. She opened shop at eight in the morning, closed at six in the evening. At night she sat on her bed and did her cutting from the patterns she carried in her head, occasionally she'd bring out the ledger book and invoices. Her older brother, Kassam, had taught her to keep books the Indian way.

Sitting there she would tell us about her childhood in Mombasa, which had been hard, or her marriage in Nairobi, where she had been happy, barring the initial abuse every new daughter-in-law received. Her first achievement was to pay off all my profligate father's debts. On a few delightful occasions she casually came up with English words none of us children had heard before. Affidavit. Mortuary. And off someone would run to bring the Oxford pocket dictionary to confirm. Yes, Mummy does know English! Better than us!

Some Sundays we would take the unpaved back roads to the new suburb of Upanga where my grandmother lived with my uncle Kassam and his family, and in the evenings we would return via dimly lit downtown streets sucking on ices we had bought on the way. And years later, when both my sisters were married and Firoz was away, minding a relative's store at Kenya's lonely but dangerous border with Somalia, Salim and I would play three-handed whist with our mother.

She had always missed my father. Standing at our doorway during Firoz's wedding, the bride and groom being received the morning following the wedding night, there had appeared sudden tears in Mother's eyes. Why are you crying, Mummy? You should be happy! And she'd say, I wish he were here. As a widow she could not perform the ceremonies required of a mother, so Naila took her place. She saw him in dreams, wearing a suit, when he would pronounce something short to her: How Firoz has grown. Pay the electric bill, dear. But as the years passed she did not mention dreaming of him, or we didn't ask. Too much was going on in our lives, final examinations, universities, sad departures, marriages.

In the nursing home, however, she saw him a few times. But our dad was now a distant memory, and her own memory was weak. What would he tell her? What she saw clearly, however, was an evil man who took away children and kept them prisoners. Where did he come from?

It was immigration that undid her, stole her away from her simple world where she was mistress and made her a prisoner in another. She became useless, a dependent, a victim. Conditions in East Africa in the 1970s intimidated many of its Asians into leaving, and Firoz was one of those who chose to go to Canada, having recently married. He and his wife set off for Vancouver and Mother followed, all three to begin a new life together. Three months later when I called her from my grad student apartment in New York, she broke down. What's wrong? There was a parrot. What parrot? A parrot can't hurt you, Mummy! Her voice was thick. She said she felt abused and she wanted to go back home. What went wrong?

She was lonely, she was hungry. There was no one to talk to. If they spoke to her they scolded her. She was crying and I could not console her. The next day she was calmer but sounded hoarse and remained adamant, she wanted to return. I advised Firoz that we should do as she asked, send her back to Salim in Dar es Salaam. He did not argue. A week later when she departed, I came rushing by overnight Greyhound to meet her in Toronto, where she had a stopover. I had last seen Mother back at home, a person of some stature, the caregiver who had brought us all up and could still hold her own as a seamstress; who had sent me abroad for my education, using all her savings for the ticket, and Salim locally to the medical school. The woman I saw at the airport gate that hot July afternoon was someone else. A woman broken—face crumpled and tearful, eyes wide with confusion, hair dishevelled—utterly defeated. Before emigrating, someone had advised her to replace all her teeth with dentures, which would be expensive in Canada, and she had foolishly done so and gained ten years; she was wearing the warm woolen coat she had saved from her younger days in Nairobi, and now she had to take it back with her and there was no room in her luggage. I can't recall with what feelings I embraced her, clichés come to mind, but that memory of her emerging out of the gate at the airport, looking grotesque and barely recognizable, stops my breath. She was fifty-five, younger than most of us now sitting beside her, egging her on to do her bit and die.

What was it about the parrot, I asked her once, some years later. "She was feeding her parrot all the time but told me I was eating too much." Her imitations of my sister-in-law Saida, cooing at her parrot, "Here, parrot, eat your foodie . . ." were actually funny. Mother spoke her mind easily. She came from a place and time where every morsel was counted, and did not understand spending resources on a pet.

A few years afterwards Mother returned to Canada with Salim, the last one to emigrate. Not happy in Calgary in the basement of his large doctor's mansion, she moved out. It was a mistake. Salim, hinting at his circumstances at home, told me, "If she moves out, she will not be able to return." Why? I wanted to ask. She's your mother! But the rejoinder was obvious, she was mine too, what was I doing about her? I preferred to live in downtown Toronto in a house too small; she would not have managed the stairs. I would have to convince my family that we should move. Excuses apart, I should face this, I had lived away from her for too many years.

But she did move to Toronto eventually, to her own apartment before ending up here.

The doctor comes, gives a quick look around the room, then lands his gaze on my mother. "Did you give her the morphine?" he asks. A middle-aged Chinese man, his hair is ruffled.

There's no expression on his face. The Filipina nurse who followed him in has gone around to the other side of the bed. "Yes," she says. "The family consented." "We should increase it," the doctor says. He could be checking inventory. He turns around and with a quick nod towards me leaves. We have an understanding.

I had already signed a guardian's consent not to revive her unless advised. But morphine is that extra step to ease her into death, because we've decided against inserting a tube through her nose to help her breathe. She would hate it, I am certain. She would say, I don't want to live under such conditions. But would she mean that? Did she understand the consent when I explained it? Had I even explained it clearly enough? The morphine seems the right decision to make, we would make it for ourselves if we had to. Still, that doubt remains, to niggle at the mind. Isn't this too easy? Haven't we been in a hurry all along? I don't want to be the one to give the final go-ahead, Yes, more morphine, let's gently push her off, but I am the son present, the decision is mine, and the rest are all happy for me to make it. They're waiting, eyes upon me. It's all right, it's what she would have wanted, but you decide. I look at the nurse and give my nod.

She's calmer, breathing steadily. Mariam, the companion, starts the prayers again. A diminutive woman, much smaller than the others, she carries the authority of experience and piety. Her open palms come together in front of her, her face pinches, and her eyes close. The others follow suit, the heads drop, the chorus begins, *Allahuma salli ala* . . . Mariam's approach has always been practical: Your mother is waiting to go; not, We should make her happy and understand her. When Mother imagined the bogeyman who captured young people and held them prisoners, Mariam advised me that the mind was gone, and the old woman would follow soon. But the mind was not gone. My mother would smile when I came, her face would gradually light up, then we would chat. Sometimes about that bogeyman. I understood exactly who it was that was following her even into death.

My second sister, Safia, made it up to high school graduation, when suddenly Mother convinced her to accept a proposal and married off the eighteen-year-old to a man fifteen years older. Why, when she knew that his first wife had left him only a couple of weeks into the marriage? He was of a wealthy family, and they made promises . . . they would take care of Safia's education, give her a better future than our mother ever could . . . and perhaps she hoped that her lot too would improve? But he was abusive, and all the promises made to us were quickly forgotten. Weeks after the wedding he hit her for not ironing his shirt properly. Mother never forgave herself. An eighteen-year-old given away just like that. My sister could have refused the proposal, but she was young and also swayed by the promises. She could have divorced him, but she stayed for the first child, who came a year later, then the next two.

This, the bogeyman who stole children.

The prayer stops, Mother keeps going. But she has slowed down. Everyone's noticed, and there's a hush in the room. The nurse has already gone.

Mum, you should see New York, I'll take you there! You'll be wowed—do you know there's a building there with more than one hundred storeys! Go on, how can that be. Really! If you say so. And I'll show you my university! All right.

She seems to have surrendered. "All right, it's time," someone says. And again the prayers begin, more frantically. I stand up and put my hand on her chest. My awkward goodbye. If only I could have expressed my love more obviously. But you knew it, Mum. I was the *laal*, after all.

There comes a commotion from outside, an unusual activity breaking the silence, and a few minutes later my brother Salim breezes in with his daughter. Officious as always—the doctor—he asks, "What's up? She's on morphine?" We nod. He goes and puts his hand on her head. She stops breathing.

An hour later, two young men and a woman from our Funeral Committee arrive and take over. We don't have to do a thing, they'll make all the required arrangements. We shouldn't go near the body, we're warned, she's theirs now. We should all go home and rest. How can I complain when it's all so convenient and easy? That's how it is, the dead dispatched swiftly and anonymously with a minimum of fuss and ritual. They're history. The next day at noon is the funeral. There are two of them, someone else has also passed away. The two funerals are perfectly orchestrated, like a military parade, and the Committee has sternly admonished the women not to weep. We believe in the spirit, not the body, is the line. And finally the short procession to the cemetery, way north of the city, snow squalls blowing around the graves. It's vast, the size of a small town, each ethnic group to its own suburb with distinct headstones. Ours, next to the Ukrainian area, are all the same compact size and austere, laid out in neat rows. The headstones are foot-square tiles laid flat on the ground, all with the same inscription, a prayer to God. No, says a member of the Committee, you cannot have your own inscription on the stone. They all have to be the same, it has been decided. Your mother's number is 1499.

MY BRILLIANT DAUGHTER

This lunch alone would have covered our month's rent once. That was way back when we first arrived in Toronto, when she was growing up on Rosecliffe Park, tall and lanky, brilliant and brazen. Now she's flown into town like a goddess on a horse and gathered twelve people around her. To greet them all at once, she said, but more likely to show off, to patronize those oldies in her family, the aunts and uncles who reached precisely nowhere in life. And look at her, how well she's done, succeeded beyond our wildest imaginings. I'll be president of IBM, she would boast. And Zera would say, Hush, you should not boast, or some devil will put a *khunoos* on your ambitions! Well, not IBM, but president of her own company is not bad. We put the world at her feet. Step on it! Go! She went. "Have some more wine, Dad!" Alcohol was haram then. Now only getting drunk is haram. A glass or two won't hurt you. When exactly do you get drunk? It doesn't matter, everything is different now. No rules left. Hell is not real. She leans over and refills my glass. Zera looks on, her face blank and judging. That's an art. She will not let the bottle near her, lest the smell pollute her. What would her spiritual master the Missionary think? Indeed what. I've told her not to tell on me that I drink a little. He's dead but guides her in her dreams and would be terribly upset. It was because he trusted me that she accepted my proposal. Way back when I went around the shops of Dar with samples of Jumbo shoes collecting orders.

If Jamila's a goddess, that other one is her prophet. Urmila. Jamila and Urmila, how nicely they fit together. Two shoes in a box. Call us Jam and Urm. Jamie and Urmie. It took me three years to realize what that meant. Zera doesn't know, though she thinks she does. So, what does a little wine matter?

"What are you smiling at?"

"Nothing."

If our daughter who's riding high wants to take us out, why not just the four of us, her family? But she must gather everyone she can, aunts and uncles and cousins. Here I am, come see me. Sophisticated, wealthy, liberated, shocking. I'll treat you at an expensive restaurant. There's a salad fork and an entrée fork, a soup spoon. A fish knife, a steak knife, a butter knife. Yes, now I know how to use them without letting the food go flying off the plate. She would kill me if that were to happen. One day she came home with a set of cutlery and trained us to use them.

Zera became totally flustered and finally gave up with, "Big spoon, little spoon? Left side, right side. What difference does it make?"

"Food is food, I totally agree," Hanif said, sounding a little too wise. "Doesn't matter how you eat it."

And Jamila flew into a rage, "You shut up!"

Not long afterwards she stopped talking to him altogether. Will not hear his name, because he had made a comment to Urmie's little sister Sharmie at a party. "No forgiveness, even for your younger brother?" Zera pleaded. "He's the only one you have, besides us!"

"He's not the only one I have. I have Urmie! Did you hear? He's nobody to me, that sexist moron! And if you go on like this, you'll be nothing to me either!"

Hanif is the only one of us not here. Zera's favourite among the two, but still, Jamila's kid brother. Isn't blood thicker than water? Or as they said back in Dar, The one who only eats with you will not die for you, but the one who shares your blood, will. Something like that. No point bringing up Dar either. If fifteen years ago I had imagined what she would be like now, this is exactly how I would have drawn her. Tall and angular, short hair, smartly dressed. Bobbing up and down with energy, shooting a look here and a look there, laughing, looking like the top of the world. But she's my daughter, I know exactly what's in her mind: Does so-and-so like me, what does that other one think, what did Mom say to you about me, did she know it was my birthday . . . It's no surprise she's got an ulcer. She didn't tell us about it, one of her cousins did, but we couldn't go to the hospital to see her, for fear of a scolding: Who told you I was here? It's nothing.

And she can read my mind. She comes over, puts a hand on my shoulder, bends over to ask, "Is everything all right, Dad?"

"Wonderful, Jamila! Everyone's happy, we all love you!"

This "love you" is a new thing too. Everyone's into "love you" now. Only lovers used to say that, do we have to say that, we who cleaned your shit?

She walks away smiling, with a sly look at Zera. She's not forgiven her mother for introducing her to one man after another, until finally she said angrily to Zera, "Me and Urmie are a couple, do you understand?" Zera managed to squeak, "Urmie?" partly in confusion, but it sounded mocking, like she was laughing at the idea, it was too ludicrous. That was it for Zera. Life sentence.

My phone rings and I walk outside to answer it, catching my daughter's sharp, suspicious eye throw a dart on my back.

"Yes, hullo, son. Yes, it's a nice party, the food is good. Have you eaten? Do you want me to bring you a takeout?"

Hanif had found a job in Madrid and was doing well. Software. In my day that meant pillows. But he explained it to me, it's like writing detailed instructions, as if to an idiot, telling a computer what to do. He always enjoyed Spanish in high school. But the Spanish economy tanked and he lost his job.

Not long after, he called us and said his wife Sonia had left him. Taken the child with her. He was crying. And so we called him home.

Your brother's back, he's unhappy, talk to him. I don't want to talk to him. He's nothing to me.

How is such hatred possible? But it is. Our parents used to say that Kaljug, the dark age, was upon us. A mother will deny her child and a daughter will abuse her mother—that's Kaljug. Well, the second part has come true anyway. When I think about it, when I look at the news sometimes, I realize that there are people who kill their brothers and even their fathers; even their daughters. In Kingston recently three girls from a family wiped out. Afghans. But we are a simple, straightforward family of four. Was the upbringing we gave them so flawed? It was not easy when we came, but we came for their sakes, we gave them love. There were the days of looking for jobs, and finally finding a menial one, at a clinic for drug addicts. Pushing trolleys of laundry. The racist remarks on the streets—*Paki go home!* The despair and humiliation. And to top everything, my public shame when a girl patient accused me of molesting her . . . and all I did was go to her assistance . . . where she was sitting on the floor crying. A picture in the *Star*. Those were hard times. If Missionary hadn't put in the money for a Coffee Time franchise, I'd have been beating the sidewalks for who knows how long, searching for "Canadian experience." Now with the old-age security for us both, it's not so bad. We paid our dues. This is a good country. Disembowels you but looks after you.

But they were always loved. Love. What more precious commodity? Jamila and Hanif. Number One, both of them—though Jamila would come up with, But I'm the first Number One.

"Dad, are you listening?"

"Yes, hullo, son. It's a bit noisy here. My mind drifts. We'll be home soon."

Back at the table, Jamila is at the head in the midst of giving a speech, while Zera is fidgeting with a fork. "Folks, allow me to publicly thank all of you who have played such an important role in my life . . . This lunch treat from Urmie and me is a small thank you!" She goes on to name Zera, thankfully, and me and her friends and cousins and uncles and aunts. And a few of her schoolteachers, one of whom is present. It is a nice gesture, but she does not name her little brother, who played with her on demand every weekend morning. Who yielded the TV control to her. And the last slice of pizza.

When it's over, as we pause outside the restaurant, rather shamelessly Zera asks, "Jamila, how much was the bill?"

Jamila grins. "Too much for you. Nine hundred and twelve dollars."

"That's almost our month's rent! But it was good, thank you. Very posh." Then, a few steps later: "Why don't you come home and meet your brother?"

The relentless mother. There's no reply. Instead, Jamila gives me a peck on the cheek—"Love you, Dad!"—and disappears, her purpose accomplished.

She loves me, regardless of my defence of her brother, but she cannot forgive her mother. Her round, short mother who speaks her mind in simple terms and loves her son too. Zera has the courage, I am the coward. When Jamila told her about Urmila, she said to me later, "She can't be my daughter." And I said to her, "I can say that but not you." The joke didn't register.

"She could have been exchanged in the hospital—remember that Arab woman in the next bed who also gave birth to a daughter?"

"Are you serious, Zera?"

In the car, on our way home, I tell her that Jamila wants me to go to Lisbon with her and Urmila.

"Why don't you go? She'll never take me anywhere . . . But you take a holiday if she's paying for it."

"What work do I do that I need a holiday? We'll go together somewhere."

We come out on Highway 7 and drive down a busy Yonge Street this Saturday afternoon, through the Iranian and Korean markets. I enjoy seeing the bright colours and the squiggles of their writing on the store signs, and the photos and names of salespeople on the billboards atop the buildings. A far cry from the days of Paki go home! Zera says I drive too cautiously, which is a fine one coming from someone who doesn't drive. The 404 is faster, no doubt, but it's too fast for me; and there's nothing to see on it but other cars, and slabs of concrete. Yonge Street reminds me of Dar, the streets I walked on as a salesman. Zera prefers Markham and Thornhill, where everything is new, clean, and large, and very quiet; where all the people we knew at Rosecliffe Park have moved. But give me Rosecliffe Park anytime, where you can walk to Maqbool's Indo-Pak Supermarket and buy bhindi or karela, or to Maqbool's chai shop next door to it for bhajia and kabab, and the 100 bus takes you easily downtown as it's always done. A lot of Muslims have moved here, men with beards and kurtas and kofias, and women in hijab and niqab, and there is the big mosque. The new Aga Khan Museum is not far away. Paki go home? This is home.

Zera puts on a CD of her master's sermons. She knows them by heart, almost, yet can't get enough of them. She's ordered twenty more from some pirate, who lists a few hundred of them in his catalogue. I loved Missionary too, but he's dead now, and how much more can you learn about your own faith? How long can you be harangued?

"Let's hear some music, Zera, for God's sake, for a change!"

"Don't be frivolous!"

"Remember that Malaika CD you liked so much?"

"No."

"Meera Bai?" That's what Missionary enjoyed too.

"After this."

It's useless to argue, but I go on all the same. Traffic's slow, there's time to kill.

"We know everything about our faith, and what's good and bad, what more is there?"

"A lot more. What he says is deep, it takes time to sink in. We have to be reminded not to be tempted by sin." She looks at me pertly.

"You're not a sinner, Zera. I know that. And do I look like a sinner to you?"

She is silent.

"Do I?"

"Keep your eyes on the road! If it were not for him . . ."

If it were not for Missionary. Yes. He was our spiritual father, and it was he who got us married in Dar es Salaam. And saved our marriage ten years later in Toronto, though she doesn't know that. We were bound by him, and we are bound by his memory. He is present in our life all the time, watching us, throwing in an admonition here, a piece of advice there. All I am saying is, we don't need him anymore. But she does.

One day while I was walking down Market Street in Dar with my shoe samples, deep in thought, a voice called out, "Ey, Nurdin!" That dry voice. When I walked into the men's shop, from where the voice came, he gave a chuckle. "Give him some water," he said to the owner. "He's a hardworking lad!" Missionary was sitting straight up as always, in the centre of the shop, facing sideways so he could look at the shopkeeper,

Kassam Hirji, on his right behind the showcase, and the street on his left. And as always looking fresh, his face beaming pink. He liked to wear long-sleeved white bush shirts despite the heat, which didn't seem to affect him, and he wore a light perfume. There was an aura to him, which made people nervous in his presence. The plump daughter of the house, having brought me water, went back to stand at the far end, where a door led inside. "Come," Missionary said to me. "What do you have there?" I pulled out a shoe sample, a cheap brown plastic sandal. Unisex. He took a quick look at it, declared, "Hong Kong," and returned it to me.

"It's cheap and very popular, Missionary Sahib," I told him. The shopkeeper asked to look at it.

"Nurdin—why are you not married?"

"I don't know . . . Missionary Sahib," I could only grin and looked in the girl's direction for sympathy, deeply embarrassed.

"Nurdin, you marry this girl," Missionary said. Just like that. "Zera is a good girl. What do you think, Kassam?" he asked the shopkeeper.

"If the boy is agreed, and his parents . . ." Mr. Hirji replied.

That was that.

Zera was his student then. I've heard her stories about the great guru of her young days countless times. And there are those CDs. His throaty voice is etched into the folds of my brain like a recording. But late at night sometimes, when she's gone to sleep, I go sit in the living room and listen to the silence. If I feel like it, I put on headphones, and quietly turn on my kind of music on the computer. Mukesh. Rafi. Talat. Lata. Romance and tragedy, songs from all those films I watched in Dar at the Odeon. Like a warm, sweet cup of chai on a rainy day.

Nurdin, you marry this girl . . . I take a quick glance at her beside me, her eyes glued to the road in front. I have no regrets. A steady companion in life is no small thing. There was that one moment, though, soon after we came to Canada. That temptation. But he arrived just in time, our master, and he saved this marriage. An answer to Zera's prayers? I don't know. Events were happening just too fast for me then, at the Addiction Centre. One thing on top of another. The Guyanese workmate egging me on to commit sin . . . a taste of pork, that first taste of alcohol, a sip of beer. That false accusation by the Portuguese girl that I touched her inappropriately . . . and a sympathetic woman called Sushila who would sit with me for coffee in the cafeteria, and then took me to her apartment one day and said, Nurdin let's get away together.

The other day I saw her again. A ghost, walking towards me on Don Mills Road, attractive in a sari, the way I remembered her. Older, but the same. The hair, allowed to grey, tied in a bun.

"Hello, Nurdin Bhai! Is it really you?"

"Sushila?"

Why pretend, when I instantly recognized her? But what a scare that was.

"Yes. Haven't seen you in years!"

"Yes . . . nice to see you again. You live around here these days?"

"St. Dennis. That one . . ." She pointed behind her.

A bright light in a corner of my life when everywhere else looked dark, with a court appearance pending, and Zera into God and guru. No satisfaction . . . there was a song with that name in those days. It completely described my condition. But then suddenly everything got resolved with Missionary's arrival, and we were all in good order. I didn't go to meet Sushila at our rendezvous as we'd planned. Bay and Wellesley, second floor. Two-bedroom. I still recall that door-hanging, the brass bells chiming as you entered. I didn't even call her one last time.

This time we didn't bother to say, See you again, we just nodded at each other and walked away. I was always a coward.

When we get home, we hasten inside. Hanif is in the living room, having fallen asleep on the sofa watching baseball. There is a bottle of pills on the coffee table in front of him. They are to help him with his headaches. Thank God it's still close to full.

Every Friday at one, the Arabic call to prayer goes out from the Rosecliffe Park mosque; a bright yellow border of parked taxis has formed in front, their Pakistani drivers having arrived in numbers for the namaz. If you ask them, they all say they are from Lahore. Not from a village near Lahore, not from Karachi. Men and boys in long shirts and caps hurry along the sidewalk, anxious not to miss the Friday prayer. We pass the cabs to reach the strip mall at the end of the street and are lucky to find a car backing out of a spot across from Maqbool's Supermarket. You have to be quick. After our shopping, our purchases in the car trunk, we go and sit at Maqbool's Halal Kabab next door. People from nearby offices flock here every day at lunchtime for the cheap thali specials. "If they come here every day, they'll get fat," Zera says, not for the first time, watching a group of young men at a table. "They run off to the gym afterwards," I reply. That's our usual joke. It's not as if we ourselves are in the best of shape. Just as we sit down, my eye falls on her—Sushila, sitting by herself at the far end, close to the window, where a loud group of Kutchi-speaking men and women have gathered. I look away. Moments later I cast a casual look towards her and see her ambling over.

"Hello, Nurdin Bhai! I haven't seen you here before."

"We come every week to shop . . . and then for a snack here."

I introduce her to Zera: "We used to work together at the Addiction Centre a long time ago. What a coincidence . . . and you live around here?"

Sushila gives me a look and says, "Yes. I moved here a few months ago only."

Zera asks, "Are you eating alone? Come and join us, bring your tray over."

Sushila does just that. And it's Zera and Sushila who do most of the talking. Zera tells Sushila about Jamila and Hanif, lies about how well both are doing and how good it is to have them close to home in Toronto. Sushila says no, she doesn't have children. "Jamila is the smart one, isn't she?" she asks, and Zera eyes her, then me. Sushila goes on, "I recall Nurdin Bhai telling me about her. She wanted to be a scientist."

"She has her own company!" Zera responds proudly. "She designs clothes."

"How lucky you are. Any prospects of marriage?—or is she already—"

"Soon now. She's found a suitable boy."

"You're lucky," Sushila says, sounding wistful, looking away. Perhaps she would have liked kids.

"It's God's mercy. We have little to do with our fates."

"How right you are."

They discuss "back there," Dar es Salaam, and where they lived. Zera above the men's shop on Market Street, Sushila behind the cobbler shop in an old house on Uhuru Street. Zera recalls the cobbler shop, it was next to Nurdin's place. She had gone there a few times and even had her feet measurements taken by the cobbler. "My father, Jairam Solanki," Sushila says, and they both get excited. He would be sitting on the floor, Zera recalls, and there was a calendar on the wall behind him, with the picture of a god on it. Sushila nods, her eyes look wet, and she takes a few spoonfuls from her bowl of bhel. They begin chatting again and discuss Gujarati foods at length.

"Why don't you come home?" Zera says. "I can show you muthia and you can tell me how to make spiced bajra roti and undhio."

It's decided.

I return from volunteering at East York General one afternoon and there's Sushila busy kneading bajra flour on the kitchen counter, Zera putting finishing touches to something on the stove. They're talking away like old chums, and I'm jealous, when I should be pleased. I sit down in front of the TV and nod off. After a while Sushila calls me to the table for tea. She puts a cup in front of me. A look is exchanged. Zera brings dhokra on a plate and calls out to Hanif to join us. He doesn't answer. She goes to his room and soon returns. "He'll eat later," she reports. The three of us have the dhokra with green chutney.

"So Nurdin Bhai, you volunteer at the hospital, how wonderful!"

"Yes, I go twice a week. Give directions to people, tell them where to go. That sort of thing."

"I think that's marvellous. I should do something like that too. And you, Zera Bai, how do you pass your time?"

Zera beams at her. "I go for yoga every morning."

"You do? Where?"

"At the community centre. Here, at Rosecliffe Park itself."

"I should come too!"

I can imagine them doing yoga and then sitting down to eat dhokra together. Why do I also imagine her looking at me, and why, when I happen to glance at her, do I feel that she has just turned her eyes away? Guilty, guilty, I find myself pleading, guilty of playing it safe and standing you up.

One afternoon while I'm sorting coupons on the table, Sushila arrives. She goes to the living room, where Hanif has been lying down on the sofa. He sits up. Zera is out shopping. It's while Sushila and Hanif are exchanging pleasantries that Hanif reveals to her that he is suffering from depression.

"Sometimes I feel like . . ."

"Like what, Hanif? You're too young to be depressed. Look at you—young and tall and handsome—and strong!"

He tells her about his wife Sonia and his son Pablito, now three years old. He misses them. Sonia left him when he lost his job in Madrid and went back to her parents in Seville. They had been happy until then. He didn't think she would return, her parents had been against the match all along, because he was dark and Muslim. Zera and I know this story, but it did not come out as fluently for us, it's a marvel how Sushila has grabbed his trust. When she takes him out for a walk, we exchange a long look and I feel completely inadequate. I would like to speak to her for a few moments. Did she wait for me that day twenty years ago at the corner of Bay and Wellesley? Does she understand? She had nothing to lose, I had to abandon wife and two kids. Does she recall what I recall . . . that afternoon in her apartment when she made me tea, and we sat on her bed. Perhaps I only imagine that . . . that possibility of sin. A different life. But Missionary arrived, and somehow I knew what I must do.

Over the next few days, Sushila comes every morning at ten and gives Hanif a head massage, then prepares a drink for him, with milk, honey, and a concoction of ground spices that she brings with her. She puts her hands on the sides of his head and chants something, and then they go out for a walk. It seems a miracle.

"What if she's working some Hindu charm on him?" Zera asks me in alarm one day when the two have just left. "I'm really worried, Nurdin. Could she be some kind of witch, a dakini who has seduced us? What do you know of her?"

"What do you care if it's a Hindu or a Zulu charm, as long as it works? And she's not a witch, Zera, she was my co-worker and now she's your friend!"

"What was she like?"

"I don't remember, but what does it matter?"

She was bright and beautiful and one day I promised to go away with her.

"If Missionary were here . . . He must have spoken about magic and so on . . . in one of his talks. I should look for the CD . . ."

"Out of a thousand CDs you hope to find one where he speaks about Hindu magic. Remember, Missionary was always broad-minded. And think of Hanif."

Whatever charm Sushila has, it also works on Zera, whose worried look soon vanishes, and the two are back to normal and do their yoga together.

Jamila calls.

"So you're not coming to Lisbon with me? You won't get another chance, Dad. A free trip at the best hotel."

"I'm needed here, beti. I have to be here for your brother. You should come to see him some time. But have fun in Lisbon . . ."

"And who's this woman who's taken over Mom's life? I have reports that she is there every day! How can you allow someone to brainwash your wife? Be a man, for God's sake!"

And so she goes on. She calls not to say hello but to harangue.

AN AFRICAN PROBLEM

In Baghdad early one morning during the time of the sultans—so the story goes—when people arrived for prayer at their beloved mosque and found a drunkard inside, slouched against a pillar, they dragged the brazen fellow out by his feet and started cursing and raining blows upon him with their slippers. But the stinking man waved them away, and with a hiccup and another attempted swig from his bottle—for the God's faithful had not dared to snatch it away lest they touch the satanic liquid—cried out to them, *Yaaro*—my friends!—if I have offended by drinking in the house of God, forgive me but show me at which place Allah does not reside!

Thus the difference between the pedant, who goes up and down on the mat five times a day lacking true awareness, and the mystic, the true lover of the One and Only who sees Him everywhere all the time. This and other stories Mulla Jamaluddin often related to his charges in the Saturday morning classes he taught at the Salam-e-deen mosque in Toronto's Rosecliffe Park. No wonder this purveyor of unorthodox ideas was often on the verge of being dismissed by the mosque's board of trustees.

I watched Mulla across the table from me in the New Safari Grill. The dingy, long and narrow room with its gritty wooden floor and dull blue oil paint was full, all its tables set against the two sides, an aisle running across the middle to the bar and kitchen; at the front stood a woman before a mike singing old Bollywood numbers to karaoke music. Yasmin, as someone called out to her, was sexy-looking in a decadent sort of way, the thin kameez tight on her full body, the makeup a bit too heavy. She had a child, a young boy, who was sitting alone at a table with a book and pencil. Now and then she would throw a glance towards him. He never looked up. There was a sadness to Yasmin as she sang to nostalgic requests with the aid of her songbook and I wondered what her story might be. My eyes trailed away from her to a tray of beer and kababs floating past me in the air. Mulla followed my mournful gaze.

Mulla Jamaluddin was my neighbour in the apartment building where I had recently moved. We had soon become friends. I was single and, solicitous of me, he often invited me to join him for tea and a chat or a meal with his wife. Sometimes he asked me to sit in on his Saturday class. He was originally from Lahore, where he had belonged to a Sufi order and—astonishingly—also been a police detective. He had come to Canada to attend a police seminar in Pembroke and decided to stay on in the country. After a year in that small town he had come down to the metropolis and was lucky to find a part-time job as a teacher at the mosque. On Thursday evenings, he also held a session of Sufi chanting at his place, which I sometimes attended to pass the time.

Mulla had been summoned to a meeting at the New Safari and he had asked me to accompany him. Appropriately, he wore his western clothes tonight, though the skullcap drew some stares. I had argued with him, in a friendly manner, If you are going to wear pants and jacket, Mulla, why top that with a "Muslim" cap and draw attention to yourself? A habit, he replied. It's like my accent, I can't change it.

I looked around the room. The fare was meat mostly, kababs and curries, the pakodas thrown in as a sop to veg cuisine. The glazed-eyed, well-heeled patrons, the women in colourful salwar kameezes, seemed familiar with each other. Now and then someone would wave at someone else or walk over for a chat. Not a face under forty; or over sixty, except Mulla—who was staring at me.

"A sad place," he pronounced.

"Indeed. But what makes you say that, Mulla-ji?"

"None of the people you see here grew up in a home where alcohol was consumed; and now they've come all the way to this dark hideaway to consume beer and whiskey with their friends."

"And kababs. They look good."

"Yes, no doubt. They are African-style, I am told—round and black, made with ground meat. These people here are mostly from Africa, though they are Asian."

"Like me."

At a table nearby, a religious argument had spun out of control. "By my mother, I will kill you!" went up an angry, somewhat startling cry. The two men, both in suit and tie, were half out of their chairs, glaring at each other like fighting bulls. The manager glided over to the table, spoke to them quietly and familiarly in Gujarati, and ushered them outside. From the door he brought back two other men, a short, dark Asian, and a lean African—a real one, not a Brownie. They walked to our table. Greetings were exchanged, the two men sat down, the waiter was called.

The African was called Martin Kigoma and he was from Tanzania; and so, originally, was his friend, Osman, who had already met Mulla previously and explained to him Martin's business. The latter took a kabab to his mouth without ceremony, took a bite from it, then—as we watched—dipped the lopped-off remainder into the coconut chutney and ate it with relish. Following which he wiped his hands and mouth with a napkin, put a hand into his black valise and pulled out two large photographs.

"Here is our man," he said. "Look at the pictures and tell me he isn't someone you know."

His manner was brisk and bullying, though friendly. He had a strong, glassy glare, and the occasional flitting glance at a passing tray betrayed a craving for a beer which he had declined out of respect for Mulla.

"Eh," exclaimed Martin over his reading glasses and passed the photos over to Mulla. "Go ahead, Sheikh, examine them."

Mulla fumbled in his pocket for his glasses but Martin pushed his own across the table. Mulla put them on and adjusted them on his nose.

The first photo was posed and showed a lean African in white bush shirt and dark trousers, standing by the driver's side of a safari vehicle looking straight at the camera; his fists were balled. The other picture had caught the same man unawares, marching in the company of a group of swaggering roughs who appeared to be singing; a few of them wore cut-away shirts to reveal their jacked-up muscles. All carried clubs or machetes.

Martin and Osman's proposition was that the man was a certain Jean-Pierre Makoya, responsible for one or more Hutu massacres in Rwanda and now posing as a Muslim called Abdul Rasheed who prayed at the Salam-e-deen mosque of Rosecliffe Park.

"It is hard to tell from a photo," Mulla murmured, looking up, passing the glasses back.

"Try, Mulla-ji," Osman pleaded.

"Try how?" Mulla asked, his voice now dry, and his face drained of the cheery brightness of a few minutes before. "Should I go and ask the poor fellow if he has committed mass murder? On what grounds?"

"Use your . . . wits, man," Martin said, sounding exasperated. "Find some way. You are known for that here, you were a detective, Osman tells me—"

Mulla laughed softly. "I'm nothing of the sort. But I do know you need proof before you can accuse a man of such a crime."

The two men sat back disappointed. Martin looked at Osman and shrugged, as if to say, What did you expect? To recompense them, Mulla ordered them beer. The bottles arrived, trailed by all the curious eyes in the long room. First a man wearing a Muslim cap, then a black man, and to top all that, two beers at our table. The look of pleasure on Martin's face told Mulla that at least for the moment he had redeemed himself. Technically he had just sinned by procuring alcohol for someone. But this Sufi was hardly ever concerned by such technical matters. It was for the conundrums he posed that he had acquired his reputation.

Now he was faced with his own puzzle.

Even if the similarity were superficially there between the man in the two photos and Abdul Rasheed, could this devotee who had become a feature of Friday afternoon mosque with his grey gallabiyah and white cap, who bowed down humbly before Allah and greeted all he met without pretension; whose wife in long dresses and hijab was equally without pretension; and who had two lovely children, could that man conceivably be Jean-Pierre, a Rwandan mass murderer? Not everything conceivable was truly possible. But then, as Mulla related in our taxi back, as a child he would hear about neighbours turning against neighbours during India's Partition. Our taxi driver, from Lahore himself, turned his head to affirm, You bet. Sometimes, as a youth, Mulla continued, after acknowledging the driver's contribution, when he saw the men of his village sitting outside the chai shop chatting, or standing outside the mosque after Friday prayer and bantering, or even when he looked at his father over a family meal, he would wonder: How did you behave in those dark days? Did you save any Hindus? Or did you help to push them out? There were empty Hindu houses and even an old temple in the village. The taxi driver turned his head to butt in, They didn't save Muslims either, on the other side. Mulla demurred, saying there were people on either side who had saved their neighbours. In his own family, however, he knew that some distant relations of his had perished in India during the Partition.

The following Friday, Mulla and I went for our weekly tea and bhajias at Maqbool's Halal. As usual I met him outside the mosque, but with him as he emerged from the gate this time was the tall figure of Abdul Rasheed. The three of us made our way to the tea shop, exchanging our first experiences of Canada. Abdul Rasheed had come via Paris four years before and worked as a teller at the Royal Bank in Flemingdon Park Mall, before being promoted to client advisor. Mulla was vague about why he had stayed on, but spoke of riots against minority sects back home. I had come as a child with my refugee parents from Uganda, and attended university in Alberta and dental school in Toronto.

Behind us a group of hotheads were dissembling loudly, apparently having just accused a man at the mosque shoe-stand of being a police spy. Their accused—or victim—was Liaqat Ali, an idiosyncratic local fellow who was well known for chatting up anyone he met, but who put them off with his excessive warmth and his British accent. People tended to veer away from his path. What made matters worse for him was that he had not quite caught on to the gestures of the Muslim prayer.

Mulla muttered, "And it was such zealots I thought I had left behind."

Our African companion smiled. He couldn't have understood Mulla, who had spoken in Urdu, but he somehow caught the gist—"Young blood. Hard to control, Mulla."

Mulla nodded. We reached Maqbool's and sought out one of the cubicles set off by blue curtains, which Mulla always preferred.

"Mr. Jamaluddin," said Abdul Rasheed, forgetting the title for a moment, and when he had caught Mulla's eye, continued, "Monsieur, I would like you to teach my children Arabic."

"Abdul Rasheed," Mulla replied quietly, a bit taken aback. "I am not an expert in Arabic."

"But you are a teacher—and you know al-Quran . . . and some Arabic, of course?"

"Yes, but . . . I know a teacher who is good in Arabic and Quran, a young man. Much better. Do you want to talk to him?"

"I want a teacher in language and religion, yes, but also in wisdom and morality—is that right?"

Mulla nodded but did not commit himself. He had thought to get to know Abdul Rasheed and learn more about him, but the man had turned the tables on him and was requesting a favour. Mulla's look wavered to the gap between the two halves of our curtain, catching the eye of one of the hotheads, who had also arrived at Maqbool's and was going on as before.

The youth, unable to contain himself, came over, and pushing through the curtain stood towering over us at our table. He wore a black vest over his white gown, and a white skullcap, and had a rich black beard.

"Mulla-ji, we should do something about that spy. He has no right—"

"To do what, Hanif?" Mulla asked in a sharp tone he rarely used.

The boy flushed and turned to depart, but Mulla continued, "And do you think the security service is so stupid as to hire a man like him?"

The boy turned and opened his mouth to speak but Mulla silenced him with the wave of a hand.

"They are more likely to hire someone who looks just like you. Keep your head on your shoulders."*

The fellow strode back sheepishly to his table, which fell silent, before antagonistic mutters arose against all heretics.

"Let me think about this, Abdul Rasheed," Mulla said.

The following day, Saturday, I was present in his class when Mulla told the children a story about a man of God called Sadruddin, who as penance for his sin of pride would hang himself by his feet over a well and ask forgiveness. The very picture of a naked mystic hanging upside down brought uncontrollable laughter into the room, as if the boys and girls had been shown a hilarious cartoon. Mulla could not help laughing too. "God forgave him," he said. "God is the Merciful." He went on to tell the kids how as a young boy, when Sadruddin was bowed in prayer, his mother would put a sweet behind him, telling him later that it was a gift from God.

As he reached the part when, one day, the mother forgot to

place the sweet in its place as usual, there was a knock on the open classroom door. Khatija, Abdul Rasheed's wife, stood there with their two children. Mulla told the kids where to sit and asked them their names. Maryam and Yunus. Like the other boys, this being the beginning of the weekend, Yunus wore a white cotton gallabiyah and skullcap. Maryam, like her mother, wore an ankle-length dress and a white headscarf. They had both brought notebooks and ballpoints.

Mulla looked up at the class, nonplussed.

"The sweet! The sweet!" came the cry. "His mother forgot to put the sweet!"

"Ah, yes," said the Mulla, eyes sparkling. "His mother forgot, but God did not forget. He put *two* sweets behind the boy's back! Remember the first line of the Quran?"

"In the name of Allah, the kind and merciful," came the chorus, in Arabic followed by English.

"Excellent," said Mulla. "He gives. And he forgives." A thoughtful look had come over his face as he said this, and he dismissed his class.

Over the loud chatter and shouting and scraping of chairs on the floor, Mulla called Maryam and Yunus over. Did they enjoy the class? Yes, they did, and they also liked going to school. They both enjoyed playing soccer and baseball. They watched soccer on TV with their father sometimes. They preferred the French teams. Yes, yes, they knew about Zinedine Zidane.

Did they recall Rwanda? No, they were born in Paris. Did they have other names? Maryam, the younger of the two, shook her head vigorously; Yunus said his mother sometimes called him Jean. That's another way of saying Yunus, Mulla told the boy to his great delight.

We walked out of the building, the two kids on either side of Mulla, holding his hands. At the sidewalk, he released them and they ran off happily.

"I see you've been talking to him," Martin Kigoma said, striding over from behind to join us. Mulla did not reply but smiled.

"He's my man, I am positive."

"You have proof now, Mr. Kigoma?"

"Circumstantial at present—but it's coming. New facts are emerging and witnesses will talk. I have videotaped our man and will show it around when I get back."

He was doing well, he said in reply to Mulla's query, he was returning to Tanzania in a few days.

"We should meet before you go," Mulla suggested. "Come home for tea . . . but no beer."

Khatija had brought the tea and cookies for us and retired.

We had stood loitering outside Abdul Rasheed's building at a little past five, and when the man returned from work and inevitably, out of politeness, invited us up for tea, Mulla accepted with a haste that was embarrassing.

"So you are teaching my Maryam and Yunus," Abdul Rasheed said. "Thank you, Mulla."

"Yes. I had no choice," Mulla said with a chortle. "But they are wonderful kids."

Abdul Rasheed nodded.

Mulla said, "I teach the Quran, but I don't need Arabic to do so. For Arabic, I suggest a young man called Akhtar. Then the children need not confuse the tedium of learning a foreign language with the spiritual message of Islam."

Abdul Rasheed looked surprised, but said, "You are wise, Mulla. Perhaps it's only the spirit of the faith that they need."

Mulla waved away the compliment. "I teach what I learned from my own teacher, a great Sufi in Lahore. His name was Noor. I have no other employment, as you no doubt know. I find great satisfaction in teaching the young."

"And the not-so-young?"

"A few of them, who are inclined spiritually. We meet for meditation and chanting."

"Perhaps I can join you."

Mulla said nothing and there fell a moment of uncomfortable silence. Finally Mulla leaned forward and said, "Forgive me for asking, Abdul Rasheed. Were you yourself born of Muslim parents?"

Abdul Rasheed's face turned a deep hue, before he recovered enough to answer slowly, "No—but there was Islam among my relations . . ."

"You accepted Islam . . ."

"During . . . after . . . the troubles in my country. Why do you ask, Mulla?"

The voice dry, without substance or pitch, as if he were hanging on to something, some redeeming notion perhaps, whatever he could call up, by the merest thread.

"And your name before . . . Jean-Pierre . . . ?"

The man's face crumpled before our eyes, a flood of tears slowly washed down his cheeks, releasing his pent-up guilt, I imagined, and easing the terrible tension of trying to live up to his new name. Mulla let the man weep in silence for some moments. Finally Abdul Rasheed sat up straight, took out a large white handkerchief from a pocket and wiped his face.

"Did you participate in any of the killings at the time, my brother?"

"Mulla . . . if you knew . . . if you could comprehend the hysteria and confusion. To be told if you did not do something, you were murdering your own people . . . they would get to you first . . . and your children . . . you were a traitor."

"They? The Tutsi?"

Abdul Rasheed nodded. "The officials, the radio. All the neighbours."

"Did you . . . yourself . . . ?"

The man broke down again. It was answer enough.

“They are on to you, Abdul Rasheed.”

“I know.”

We met Martin and Osman again at that den of intoxication and nostalgia, the New Safari Grill. This time Martin did not observe any niceties out of respect for the man of God: he drank liberally.

“We in Africa are determined to bring our criminals to justice this time, Sheikh.”

A tall order but a good cause, Mulla observed. The continent had suffered much recently . . . it needed hope and honest leadership. He could say the same thing about the country he came from, high up on the world corruption index. And here he was himself, pleading the cause of a confessed murderer.

“The Africans of South Africa have taught the world a lesson in nobility and forgiveness—”

“Have they, my friend? Have they truly forgiven? That’s what the world would like to believe, the world that enslaved us for so long and is fearful of our vengeance.”

“There are other criminals on your continent—everywhere—who do not have to pick up a weapon—”

“We have to start somewhere, Sheikh. Are you suggesting that laws, the justice system, can be made flexible—left to the whims of individuals? Where is deterrence, where is justice? Crime and punishment, Sheikh.”

"I don't know, Mr. Kigoma. I simply wonder if repentance in this case is not enough. The man still has to face his God daily. And there are the lives of the two children. Should they pay a price?"

"Countless children in Africa pay a price every moment, Sheikh."

A few weeks later, Abdul Rasheed took a flight for Arusha, Tanzania, to be questioned by the prosecutors of the Rwanda tribunal. His family saw him off at the airport. As did Mulla Jamaluddin and I.

TOVA IN TEL AVIV (YOU WOULD LOOK AWAY)

My Friend.
It's drug mischief that's brought you up in the mind . . . so painful. Or I would not trouble you. Again. It was so long ago. I betrayed you then . . . you couldn't have forgotten that. I see a boy walking diffidently up the curving hill of United Nations Road, Dar es Salaam, eyes fixed on the ground in front of him. The stupefying African heat, the brilliant daylight. What do you see? Where might you be now?

You would look away into the sun's glare, determined to avoid me, your face scrunched up, and when you could bear it no longer you'd turn your head back, just in time to miss me passing in that glorious blue Citroën ID like a princess in a chariot. But one day our eyes met. I had you. Do you want a lift? I said. How did I sound then? Wonderfully sweet, I bet. And the shy dark boy dripping sweat allowed himself just one step closer, to sink his eyes in mine, and spoke in a dry voice—No thank you—and walked on. Your heart went thump, thump, thump, I could feel it. And mine? It had stopped. I could not believe it. Just a lift? Just a lift. The next day you were not there, and the whole week following, my driver Abdu sneaking sly looks at me in the mirror as I scanned the sidewalk. I, who was the insulted party. You were teasing me? No. Shy, you said, only shy—I was so embarrassed. That was when you did finally appear and accept the lift. Almost tripped in the process, I stifled a laugh. Where shall the driver drop you? Just there, opposite the mosque is fine. You live here, near the mosque? No—yes, just close by. You didn't want me to see your home, did you? And me, naive European girl, couldn't understand why. How nervous you looked, each time we let you out, and without even a look behind, you ran for your life!

You're so white; I mean—not *pink*.

Is that what you first noticed about me? Not pink?

No—that hair—no, before that—

Yes?

The car—it's so majestic, the best car on the road.

You noticed the car first and not me?

But your hair—blazing, like a fire!

Flatterer. Yes, the brown head of curls, and the green eyes, how could you have missed them in the Citroën. My eyes are dimmer now, the hair is short and black; fashions change; and yes, dyed; and yes, thin too. You actually didn't know where I came from. Sweden, you said once, and I pretended it was true; you didn't know the flag on the car hood, the blue and white with the star in the middle that had been the badge of my people for so long, and how that endeared you to me. European, sure, but Romanian refugee, smuggled out through the border aged two.

I had not a friend in town, and this boy comes along; shy, serious, thoughtful. That's the first thought that came to mind when I saw you—What is he thinking in that head? And he's had his hair cut. It looks funny. And dark, he doesn't care about the sun roasting him, turning him darker. His skin will wrinkle sooner, Mama might have said. I told her I had met this nice student from the boys' school who had agreed to teach me Kiswahili, and after some discussion she and Papa agreed. You can bring him after school on Saturday... The first time you came to our house you fell from the rattan chair. I laughed, I cried—for you. Almost everybody fell from that ill-designed chair, how could you have known. I could have warned you but didn't. Forgive a girl her whimsy.

You taught me calculus, my friend, I taught you Shakespeare; you did my physics for me, I gave you tennis . . . And when I said let's sit out in the sun and came out in the balcony in my bathing suit, your brown face turned maroon.

I am sorry. But you did borrow my mother's *Lady Chatterley's*; just to find out what the fuss is about, you said. Sure. That too. I told her I had been reading it and a friend had borrowed it.

Certainly there was the exotic to you; the dark. And I was lonely. Not that there wasn't other game in town. Little, but there. Hofner, also from Israel; the American twins who arranged a tryst under

Selander Bridge to do the dirty on us diplomats' daughters. But you were my special; your name I'd say over and over at night, happily; a king's name; no, an imam's, you insisted . . . precious music in my memory, *Hoo . . . ssen, Hoo . . . ssen* . . . until that scud-firing monster came along in Iraq and put his stamp on it.

The war came in Sixty-seven. And we were non grata, more or less, more because of my father's job. He was a spy. African governments did not like us anymore. And you never saw that Citroën again. I disappeared. No goodbye, no notice. How rude, how heartless. But not heartless, please believe me. Simply, no choice. What's the point, Mama said. You are going far away where he can never belong. And you are both young. Etcetera. What I might have told my own children later. And you yours.

It's the drugs, you see, that have stirred you up like some genie. Yesterday I saw a boy blow himself up into shreds of bone and flesh and here I am. I am well, just shock, but it's the drugs. The boy's face. And this precious thought: I wish I could send it to you, this thought of love and friendship; this sorry apology. I wish I could write it before it disappears. Again.

Tova

Tel Aviv

"Will you sign the petition? This proposed boycott of Israeli investments—not that it will make any difference, but still."

"Yes, if enough people sign it, it could make a dent."

"There's an article here says that an inordinate number of Jews make up the warmongering neocons. Does that make sense?"

"Well, if the Arab countries are crushed and pushed back ten years, that's to Israel's advantage . . . But I feel uncomfortable. There's a difference between Jew and Israel."

"I agree, but . . ."

"You know, all my professors—those I recall—were Jews? Let's see—Julius Goldstein, Abe Klein, Ralph Amado, Jay Hirshfield . . . I looked up Hirshfield online recently, he's still there. He and his wife invited me to their house for a barbecue one summer . . . I wonder if I should contact him. I didn't even know then what a Jew was. Innocence lost."

"Yes, innocence lost."

It was a few days after the Munich massacre, the 1972 Olympics. Balmy July afternoon in New Haven, in the backyard. I recall her standing behind my chair, Mrs. Hirshfield, a bowl of salad or something in her hands. Friendly, curious, so informal. And so American. I was still new in the country, sitting with a few undergraduates, graduates, one postdoc and the prof. I had declined beer. Yes, I'd been watching the news, I told her, and how tragic it was, the senseless killing at the Olympics, what was the world coming to? What value to life?

"Do you recall the first time you fell in love?"

"I don't know . . . I think so."

"You never told me!"

"What difference does it make? You never told me about your past either. We met, and that was the beginning. Year Zero."

"You don't remember anything? I can tell you do."

"There are some things we dare not touch."

They are there, precious and delicate. I'm afraid if I touch them they'll break and fall away, ashes. I want to preserve them. The beauty, the laughter. The ice-cold Coke your mother brought in glasses, such a delicacy and she knew how much I enjoyed it. And she brought us peanuts, shelled, and you Tova recited *Romeo, Romeo* . . . Tova. What a lovely name. Where would you be? I looked you up, many times, not to contact and harass you but just to see if you're there, somewhere. Safe. Would you remember, in any case, the uncouth brown boy who fell off the rattan chair . . . yes you would. Then why disappear? I came to your flat, twice, knocked, until the neighbour said, They've gone away. In a taxi, to the airport. Hussein. Did you learn to hate that revered name later? Every time I read of a bloody incident over there, a rocket or bomb or something else, I cannot help seeing you.

Hussein

Markham, Ontario

—

My Friend.

Hussein, then. Why do I think of you? It's the drugs. The shock. The wet spot on my cheek that I cannot forget. A tiny piece of the boy. I felt it then, its impact, but when I awoke it wasn't there. Perhaps I imagine it. A piece of flesh. A drop of blood. I shudder… But why you? I've had lovers, two of them, real ones, and the marriage. They've all rushed to see me. Family and friends. Son and daughter. Former lover. But it's you, falling off the rattan chair and I laughing my best laugh ever. Never like that again. How innocent we were. I want to cry. I cry. Do you ever think of me? Please think of me. Think of me. First love, no? First love, yes…

Mama's smile when we came out of my room. The anxious look. Switching from one to the other, question on her face.

What does he say? I would like to hear what he says. You don't have to keep him all to yourself, your door closed?

I don't want you to listen when we talk.

All right. But—

She didn't finish.

Why does she have such a tragic face? you asked.

Tragic? I laughed. But you were right, tragic indeed. Your face tightened, you made a claw, raised it to your face and brought it down. I knew what you meant, she had hollows on her face as though the flesh had sunk in some places.

Like someone died.

She lost her mother and father. And a brother. In the war.

The Second World War? But that was long ago.

You didn't ask how they died, thankfully. Who wanted to go into that?

Do you want to kiss me? You never want to kiss me?

I leaned forward. All you could come up with was a squeak: Kiss?

Here. I pointed. Slowly you kissed me on the proffered cheek. I offered my lips. I leaned further forward, looked into your eyes. After an infinity you touched yours to mine.

Enough, I said, as though you knew how to go further.

And later my mother at the door with that grief look. Like someone died. Sit down, she told you. Would you like another Coke? You glanced with horror at that chair and said, No, thank you . . . very much. And we laughed, Mama and I. Not at you. Yes at you. But not derisively, my friend. As though we ourselves spoke the Queen's English. Just at how funny everything could be. You see, you made her laugh too. No small thing.

Your Tova

"Why that distracted look? You're not paying attention."

"What do you mean?"

"I just showed you the number of votes for the boycott, by country. France and Germany are the highest."

"That may be time-dependent. It may change."

"Still thinking about that first love?"

"What first love? Don't be silly."

Yes, I was. But why now, all of a sudden? What prompts a single memory of the past just to crop up?

"When we talk like that, it's as if we don't have a present."

She smiles at that and goes away for her nap.

That kiss. It stayed with me for days. I could think of nothing else. What do you mean days, you're thinking of it even now. How sweet it was. But what do I remember of its sweetness? It's what I told myself, how beautifully sweet. I don't want to eat or drink, so as not to lose that taste. So that's what they do in the movies. But in the movies they linger. Is she making fun of me? What a nice girl, this Beautiful Name. That's what I called you, Beautiful Name. Tova. Your other name, you said once, was Rosa Mihaela. But don't ever call me that, you said. If you do, I will hit you. But why not, and why did you tell it to me in the first place? Your father swam across a river to escape Romania, you said. And you? You didn't remember. I always imagined you on a red passport that said Rosa Mihaela.

Your father. Bald and dumpy, sitting in his chair quietly, beside a pile of newspapers. His head buried in one. You read the Hebrew ones for him. He didn't know it, you did, because you took lessons, Thursday, from an old lady in town, before your judo lessons. Why judo? We laughed. You wouldn't show me the moves, because you would have thrown me and you didn't want to do that. One day you gave me a copy of *Doctor Zhivago* to read, your silent father's suggestion. And another time James Baldwin's *Another Country*. And they both told you to go with me to see Shakespeare at the Odeon. I was embarrassed, insisted we get down from the Citroën a block away and walk to the cinema, you ahead. You went inside first, then I followed. To be seen with a girl, and a white girl at that! I would have been teased no end. I didn't understand the films, recall Brando giving a speech and Olivier jumping about. Didn't even know these actors by name. Just those two movies and then I found excuses not to go. The second time, before I came to join you inside, someone else had slipped in beside you, and made lewd comments throughout, you said, and you would never forgive me. I didn't either. Still don't, for my cowardice. But they would have said I was chasing you because you were white, and they would have called you names. Free. Easy.

Sorry, Beautiful Name. Where would you be now, doing what? Did you join the army, with your judo? Did you kill anyone? Google doesn't know you—Tova Jacob? No Rosa Mihaela either. Do you only exist in my imagination? They say memories can be manufactured . . . A golden-haired Israeli girl in a blue Citroën on United Nations Road. No. I kissed her, ever so lightly, the taste so sweet, so sweet. And then . . .

Hussein

"That suicide bomber," he says, and she looks up.

"Yes, what?"

"How many died?"

"Three people were killed and the young bomber."

"What a waste."

"A lot more were killed by the Israeli planes. An entire family."

His heart sinks. What a world we came out into. What have we become.

Hussein.

My heart is weak, they say. That's why they're watching me. The shock of the explosion. The sight of blood. But it's my gut that's torn, I tell them, it's the gut that burns even if I wasn't hit, I was too far away to be hit. I only saw. The boy blew himself up. We've repaired it, they say. Your gut. And with the medication the pain will go away.

They've repaired it. Medication.

But you won't go away. Like a djinn you've sprung up. Why is it, after so long, my mind latches only onto you? Okay, the kids and grandkids, they are there, but then it's you. I asked to look into my old album with these poor eyes, but I could not find you. Not a trace. Did Mama remove you? Someone else? Myself? The only proof from that time, something I could touch, thrown away into rubbish. Vanished. I cried. It's only this memory now that is my album . . . that plays like a movie and I don't know if it's old or new.

The sight of the pretty nurse brought rude thoughts into my mind just a moment ago. I imagined her love life. Why are you smiling? she asked. I imagined you in a bikini, I said. You don't object? No, of course not. Sometimes I like to come out in a bikini.

When I came out in the swimsuit, not a bikini, just to shock, you stared but didn't stare. Looked away carrying that image. Red with blue and white stripes diagonally across. Red, your face. Red, mine.

You can look. It's a swimsuit.

I know.

Look, it's okay.

He turns. And stares. Up and down. Breathless. I sit down, stretch my legs towards him.

Well?

Nice. You look nice.

You want to touch? He's helpless. Anywhere. Touch me anywhere.

Anywhere. He reaches out a trembling hand, his finger goes up and down the cleft.

You can kiss me on these lips, I say.

Your Tova

Where would you be now, Tova? Would you remember, in any case, the uncouth brown boy who fell off the rattan chair . . . yes you would. Of course you would. We made something out of nothing. You started it.

Perhaps you joined the army and were killed, I thought. And I thought perhaps you went to live in a kibbutz. No, not her, I said. Maybe you moved to New York and are right now not far away at all. Two people connected by thought. Memory. Can thoughts find each other, grope and play and caress, over a distance? Like two magnetic fields? Give pleasure in some abstract space? But what would you remember? Perhaps I've imagined that kiss. Memories change, they say. No, and there was the second kiss . . . The even more deadly one.

Hussein

I saw your home, my friend, which you didn't want me to see. Let's pass his home, I said to Abdu. I don't know it, he said. Find it, I told him angrily. He smiled. The next day sure enough we drove by your house, a row house, actually, in a square block. There was a yard in front, two papaya trees. The door was open but it was too dark inside to see. A woman went in with a boy. I knew you gave lessons, it must be your pupil with his mama.

I felt I violated you, by peeping into what you did not want me to see. I did not want to tell you I had seen your home, you would have stopped coming to mine, and I would have lost you . . . Did we do wrong? When I said, My turn to touch, and held your hardness and you wet your pants instantly, in a flood. And the smell. You left quickly, holding a magazine in front of you and I rushed to the bathroom and smelt my hand. I licked it.

And then we left. Twenty-four-hour notice, Papa said. And I forgot. Of course I forgot. Please remember me, Hussein, wherever you are. Clever boy, he will go away, Mama said. Remember me, bring me back, remember me . . .

Tova

Dear Professor Hirshfield,

You may not remember me, but I spent a summer in your lab when I was an undergraduate. It was 1972, and I worked on feedback stabilization of plasmas. I found you on Google and thought I'd send you my greetings. That was a most enjoyable summer for me. And very instructive. Please give my regards to your wife. And my thanks for having welcomed me.

Sincerely,
Hussein Nanji

"I had a most disturbing dream."

"Yes? What was it—do you remember?"

"Yes, clearly this time. It's really depressed me. We were in some country travelling in a tourist bus, and we were stopped at a border area. The police singled out you and me, took us to two different buildings. I don't know why they singled us out. There was a guy with a moustache in charge. They took me to a room and waterboarded me, and while they were doing that, this guy with the moustache took out his belt, tucked in the buckle, and was ready to whip me, and I kept protesting, But why? And I realized there was no sound from your end. I was scared. At that time two helicopters descended outside, some men in uniform came and took away the guy with the moustache. You see, I had given my phone to a person in the bus, and he must have called Toronto. You were okay."

"That's a frightening dream. I heard you shout a couple of times in your sleep."

"When I woke up, I thought, how little we know of what people go through in other parts of the world. How much they suffer. We read about it, but we don't really know. We can't know, sheltered as we are, covered in a blanket. That's what I thought . . . and still think. How sheltered we are. How little we know."

"Isn't it good to be sheltered? To have been saved?"

"Yes."

HOW TO LIVE LONGER

He reaches out and hands me a peanut, then pops one into his own mouth. I return a smile, for he means well, our food monitor. Or should I say, our health monitor. He wants to make sure we'll be together for as long as possible. We're at our daily quality time, when we sit on the couch in the evening and watch a movie before going to bed. A comic street scene in Mumbai with a mouthwatering display of Indian sweets is the cause of our distraction. "Would you like a sip of my water?" he gestures to the bottle on the coffee table. "No thanks, Zool. But I'll go and make myself some chai." He starts to say something but thinks better of it. He would like the tea, but disciplined as he is he will resist. He takes a pinch of sesame seeds to follow his solo peanut and places the nut bowl back on the table. I put the movie on pause and walk to the kitchen and prepare the masala chai, adding a surreptitious half teaspoon of sugar. That can do no harm, surely. Reflected in the microwave door, I don't look too bad. Rather proud of myself, lost sixteen pounds already in the last year. But Zool's lost forty, and he's a new man. I pull out the cookie jar from its shelf and grab a saffron-topped nankhatai, dip it in the chai until it's just so, and take a nibble. It's gone just in time, the sweet taste still teasing the mouth as Zool walks in, using the break to take a quick jaunt through the downstairs rooms. A round is exactly ninety-six steps; he makes ten rounds every night, adding four steps each time for an even thousand. That's in addition to the yoga at six in the morning, the cycling at ten, the evening walk, and going up and down the stairs throughout the day. I always join him for the walk, four thousand and ninety-six steps exactly. He likes that number. It's the sixth power of four. He was an engineer.

He takes a fleeting look at the cookie jar, which I forgot to put away, but says nothing and I pretend not to notice. I'm still thirty pounds over from ten years ago but—not something to tell him—does it matter? I'm a grandmother now. And healthy. But when Zool reached that magical—I should call it cursed—milestone of sixty, his attitude towards life changed. During the surprise birthday party that I arranged for him, he was unusually reserved and hardly ate. The party was a mistake, he did not enjoy being reminded of his years. Since then he's like the cautious driver on the road, always nervous about getting hit. His friends are the same, and they compare their bp, sugar, and cholesterol levels as jealously as they would compare their grades back in school.

"Look at us," he said to me one day, soon after that party. "We were as handsome as a film couple. They called you Nutan, and me Ashok Kumar. We were trim and fit. We played badminton, we swam. What's happened to us?"

We also sang love duets at parties. What happened was that the kids grew up and left. The house had been paid off, and there was change to spare. We were less active, enjoyed food, and the pounds sneaked up until we were what our mothers used to call "healthy." We had always loved to eat. My cooking was a sensation anytime, just like my mother's back in Meza, the town on the coast of Tanzania where we grew up. Here in Toronto, people will call me up sometimes with an order for a biriyani or a trifle pudding for a party. I decline. I no longer cater, as I did when we first arrived in Toronto and had no jobs. Look, I reply, I'm writing a cookbook, wait for it. It will have all our classic recipes and more. I should have finished it, before Zool pulled me by the hand after that birthday party to stand with him in front of the hallway mirror. "Look." He patted his stomach a few times like a drum, lifted a fold of flesh and let it drop with a wobble. He eyed my waistline but knew better than to put his hand on me then. "Look," he said. "It was not there before, it should not be there now." He revealed to me the result of the long hours he'd spent buried in his study the past several weeks. It was a complete program for living healthy called ELMO—eat less, more often.

He'd done the numbers. If we followed his program, Zool said, we would live longer minus those extra pounds. And so I put aside my best recipes for biriyani, kuku paka, and gulab jamun. If you eat them in micro quantities, you might as well forgo them. Food is to be relished. But Zool's numbers were right and he is back to his Ashok Kumar look—trim straight figure, thin moustache, cropped curly hair (though dyed), and our women friends already cast glances at him. I worry sometimes.

"You should get a tummy tuck," he said one day.

"No way," I replied. "I'll lose weight my own way."

"Look at Moez and Sara. I'm sure she's done it, and they both had facelifts during their so-called trip to Thailand. Do you notice how their faces have that gleaming look?"

"Yes, but his is also more creased. And she can barely smile."

"You say you'll lose it and you don't and then you complain you don't fit into your winter coat."

"It's twenty years old!"

He knows I would love to fit into it again, a pure wool, royal blue, full-length coat. He is helping me get there.

I return to the living room with my tea and let him have a sip. He will not have more, and so much the better, masala chai is not something you squander. Some things you can't give up, or life's not worth living. I don't know how I've been able to give up so much good food. Cooking is an art, they say. It's an art I no longer practice. "We're losing our culture!"

I protested one day. He wouldn't budge. I thought the culture bit would get to him, hung up as he is on our lost history as Asians in Africa. Before ELMO he was obsessed with collecting family stories about back there. Mostly fantasies, in my opinion, but that didn't bother him. How someone's grandmother fought off a lion in Tanzania outside her home, that one's ancestor was hanged by the Germans for spying, someone else's father assisted the Mau Mau fighters in Kenya. People were only too happy to provide them for him. That collection is now posted on the internet. Since retiring, my husband has desperately needed to keep occupied.

The film we are watching is *Dabangg*, with Salman Khan with the ripped body. When I watch him I get the shivers. Zool is nowhere like him, but then Ashok Kumar too looked different. In those days actors didn't have ripped bodies, they were more your romantic, handsome gentlemen who serenaded pretty ladies with love songs. And Zool was romantic and a gentleman. He sang, I was pretty.

Back in Meza, boys and girls always hung around separately. We had eyes for each other, of course, and there were the rumours and the teasings and the love letters passed on by the "interpinters"—our go-betweens. One afternoon I was delayed in school and found myself hurrying behind my gang, who were well on their way home. The trail was muddy, mango trees all around, and the occasional baobab looming above, looking as if its head were buried in the ground. Soon dusk would fall, and the djinns would emerge. Meza is an ancient Swahili town known for its hauntings. There are many stories I could tell about that. Just as I buckled my school bag and prepared to make a dash to join the girls, whom I could hear chattering in the distance, someone emerged from behind a tree, giving me the scare of my life, and started walking beside me. Immediately I started whispering the naad-e-ali, the most powerful prayer there is and for emergencies only, but I recovered, seeing it was Zool, and found myself blushing deeply.

"Mr. Moses wanted to see me after school and so I got delayed," I explained to him. Mr. Moses was our English teacher from India. He liked me and would detain me for the lamest of reasons, and I would be flattered. But he never laid hands on me. It was said that he was a Jesuit. I don't know if that explains anything.

Zool was walking quietly beside me, looking ahead. He wore a cloth shoulder bag of books and idly played with a shiny cricket ball in one hand. After about a minute of silence between us, I glanced at him curiously, which startled him, and he said quickly but quite softly, "I love you."

"What did you say?" I replied after a moment.

"Anita, I want to say I love you."

We continued walking, as normal. What did he know of me? Enough, I guess, we came from similar families, our fathers ran businesses in our small town, his a grocery store, mine a clothing store. We attended our prayer house, the khano, regularly. I admired another boy at the time, about whom the girls teased me, but Zool was here with words of love, and he was handsome.

"Let me think about it," I said primly, not losing a step, but my heart was pounding. I felt nervous and afraid and elated at the same time. Certainly none of my friends would have had anyone declare to them so openly that he loved her. That happened in films, both Hindi and English. I love you! What a bold statement! I felt privileged. That night I had a hard time falling asleep, debating with myself: yes or no? The next day at school when Zool and I passed each other and he raised an eyebrow at me, I smiled at him and said softly, "Okay." I forgot about the other boy, who had been only a fantasy. But that's not completely true.

Soon everyone knew about us, our families, friends, and neighbours, and even our teachers. We were the lovebirds of the town. It surprises me now that no one raised objections to our daring. We would wait for each other after school, sometimes taking the long and lonely walk back home, past the German war cemetery with its broken mildewed graves. Sometimes we did our homework together. He was always good in math, I in geography and history. After high school we both went to university in Nairobi on government scholarships. No one else attracted either of us, we simply remained together, in love. And we are still together.

After we finish watching the film, I go up to bed and he goes to his study, which is our older boy's former bedroom. He will work for one hour, then return downstairs and walk two times round the rooms to complete his thousand, and come up to bed. He has no problems sleeping.

Our friend Moez, also from Meza, has taken the India route to health and longevity. There's been a rivalry between him and Zool ever since they were in school. It used to be grades, now it's the wellness quotients. Who tackles his numbers better. They've always had their distinct ways, just as back then, when Zool entered the science stream and Moez went into commerce. Moez is the wealthier one now, he drives a Mercedes to our more modest vehicle, and walks with a swagger. A show-off. At restaurants he will chat up the servers and call out the chef; he will speak to other tables, blind to their annoyance. And when he finds his body getting the better of him, when the paunch becomes pronounced and stairs are a strain, he will check in at the Amarapur Clinic in Kerala. The first thing they do to you there is take away all your pills; then on it's hunger, enemas, yoga, meditation, and daily long walks. The Enema Games, I call it. The first time Moez returned from Amarapur, after a month's stay, he had shrunk, having lost twenty pounds. Is that really you, Moez, we joked, or are you his younger brother? It was as if he had time-travelled back to his youth, while here we were, his friends the ageing heavyweights. He had even shaved off his moustache and dyed his hair jet black. But to tell the whole truth, that face had lost its distinction, it was a baby face with creases. Still, there was all this new energy in him to do something new and exciting. Tour vineyards, go to the Shaw Festival, try a new restaurant in Collingwood. It took him two years to regain the weight, then he set off for Amarapur once more to be serviced.

Sara doesn't check in with him but meets him later somewhere like Bangalore or Goa. They take a big tour together and, possessed by cravings, he binges, as Sara let out quietly once. Fish turns to seafood, and he gorges on shrimp, crab cakes, and lobster. In the right company, he'll attack a lamb shank. But Sara herself eats like a bird and she exercises and looks years younger than me, though I'm sure it's Botox and tummy tuck too. And lots of makeup. They both have personal trainers. How can they not live forever? I am jealous, that should go without saying.

"When we're both dead," I said to Zool, "these two will smirk every time they remember us . . . We should go to Amarapur." He refused. He's an engineer, and what they can do there, he says, he can do here. And cheaply. "I can figure it out. Don't worry, Anita. We're going to be around yet . . ."

Zool's weight plan, ELMO, is actually based on common sense, it sounds like advice that my grandfather used to give. Eat anything, but eat less and frequently and your body will learn to crave less. I stopped reminding him of my dear bapa after the first couple of times, when he didn't see the humour. He is right, of course, ELMO is a complete system and not just folk advice. He provides exercise and activity regimens. If you follow it, your sugar levels, blood pressure, and cholesterol will plummet and so will your weight. Guaranteed. You'll feel younger. It's all described with impressive numbers and charts in a slim volume he uploaded on Amazon, for sale at $1.99, proceeds to go to our alma mater, Rustomjee High School in Meza. We're still attached to where we come from. Where he declared his love to me. There's a bonus chapter on how to manage your retirement. It became a bestseller in its category.

I'm proud of my Zool, really. He's low on the humour quotient, but he's sensible. With that scientific mind of his, he can make any subject look easy.

Even poetry, who would believe? He's not a poetry person, even novels he disdains, but one day a few months ago while surfing the net he came across "Ode to a Nightingale" by John Keats. "Listen to this, Anita," he said, coming halfway down the stairs, and read it out aloud. We had studied it in school under Mr. Moses, and it all came back, that excitement of discovering poetry, the teacher declaiming it in his throaty voice. That night during quality time, we sat down and discussed the poem instead of watching an Indian movie for the nth time. And just like that, poetry became Zool's new obsession.

I would hear him recite a verse aloud to himself, repeat it over in different ways, sometimes a few lines. Occasionally a single word would explode behind his closed door. "Hark!" He was like a scientist examining specimens, or Archimedes when he made his discovery. Finally, after a day of blissful silence for me, he came down for breakfast and announced his golden rules for writing poetry. His method is called FIRM, for Feeling, Invention, Rhythm, and Metaphor. *Be a Firm Poet* also went on Amazon, though it was not a bestseller. Poetry can't compete with weight loss, for sure.

Zool and Vyas had an argument regarding poetry one evening. Vyas is the third member of our trio of geniuses and fast friends from Rustomjee High (or Secondary, as we called it) School. As luck would have it, they were chosen to go to different universities, Zool to Nairobi, Moez to Dar, and Vyas to Kampala. They came to Toronto soon after graduation, the year following Idi Amin's expulsion of Asians from Uganda. In those days when you came to Canada you took whatever job you were offered, usually well below your qualifications: Zool became a draughtsman in a government surveying office but rose up eventually to become senior engineer in the highways department; Moez, after a year as a teller in a Bank of Montreal branch downtown, went into real estate and made a fortune; Vyas became a Toyota salesman and is now a partner at the same dealership that took him on. But he's always been a literary soul, ever since our school days. He missed his calling, as many did who emigrated.

Moez and Sara had organized a ghazal program, showcasing the Indian vocal maestro Pandit Shivkumar from the city of Agra. The recital was by invitation only, at a banquet hall in Markham well known for wedding receptions. It was a bitterly cold night in December, a week before Christmas; everywhere looked desolate, and snow squalls swirled on the roads like dancing dervishes. Still, most of our friends and acquaintances were present, dressed in their finest Indian costumes.

Pandit Shivkumar is a favourite of Moez's and he invites him from India whenever he gets the craving for culture, which is about once a year. Moez says there is no one to compare with Pandit on the Indian classical music scene. We never knew such music back in our little town, but Moez now claims authority, and we humour him. The buffet was very good that night but the wine was poor. But for most people we know, wine is wine, usually red and Shiraz. There were a few Johnnie Walkers under the counter, reserved for Moez's friends. Zool and I sat at a table with Vyas and Yasmin. After we had queued up for the food and sat down, the MC came forward and welcomed the singer with heaps of flowery praises. Pandit looked on and smiled humbly where he sat on the floor. When the MC had finished, Pandit joined his hands and began his flattery. He thanked Moez and Sara, his patrons and great connoisseurs of music, and thanked the enthusiastic and knowledgeable audience. He then nodded to the tanpura player, who began to play the drone, and himself started with "O Canada" on the harmonium and received warm applause. With a grateful smile he adjusted his posture and began to sing ghazals, one after another, all favourites with those present. Slowly people dragged their chairs forward to be closer to the maestro. And at our table, Zool and Vyas started their argument.

As the audience began to clap their hands and rock ecstatically from side to side, Vyas began muttering, "Is this poetry—'your house and my house,' 'you are the candle and I am the moth'? What do these people know about ghazals? They applaud everything, and he patronizes them. He must take them for idiots."

"There are actually a few very simple rules to writing poetry," my husband put in slyly, taking his cue here to make a plug for his new obsession. "FIRM," he said with glazed eyes and held up four fingers as he began to explain. Both men had had a few glasses of Scotch, neat, and Johnnie Walker loomed ominously over our table. "I know that, but . . . !" Vyas would start, as Zool drawled on, oblivious. He does tend to go on nonstop after a few glasses. I said, "Zool, he knows that. Don't forget, he was our poet in Meza. And be quiet now." My dear husband believes that he discovered America when he placed his right foot on the runner at the Toronto airport. Or, as Moez once said, Zool would try to teach Newton the laws of gravity. It goes this way, Isaac.

Pandit was taking requests, the guests sang along, the MC was showing off his Urdu, having spent a few years in Pakistan. It all sounded false. Vyas is so right, I told myself, if also drunk.

But I had blundered when I said that Vyas *was* a poet. Our looks met no sooner than I'd uttered those words, and I saw his face turn blank, his lips tighten. I had lit a match and soon enough he exploded. He stood up awkwardly. Unsteady on his feet, in an edgy voice, a finger pointing towards the singer, who was now sitting in the midst of his adulating audience, he uttered, "Excuse me . . . excuse me, Pandit Shivkumar. Yes—do you call this poetry, what you are singing to this ignorant mass . . . these trivial love couplets full of age-old clichés . . . ? Hein?"

The hall fell silent, as though the soundtrack had suddenly switched off. Then someone who did not show his face spoke up, "You ass, who are you calling ignorant?" "Who does he think he is? A poet?" "Some fool from Toyota . . ."

Pandit merely smiled like Buddha where he sat.

"Yes!" shouted Vyas. "A real poet! A living poet!" And he stormed out, followed by Yasmin, who threw a helpless look behind at me. I followed them in a hurry, even as Zool opened his mouth to restrain me.

I had grabbed my coat. And Vyas's, and Yasmin's. The chill outside felt like a sword through me, I gasped for breath. "Here!" I managed to shout to the wind. Yasmin stopped and gratefully put on her coat, and ran after Vyas with his.

We reached their Camry and I went to sit behind them in the back seat. Yasmin turned to me with pleading eyes. "He's in his mood."

"What's the matter, Vyas?" I asked him. "You know what these concerts are like, why spoil it? And you shouldn't take Zool so seriously. He needs a hobby, and . . ."

Poetry had been Vyas's passion. In Uganda, where he went to university and met Yasmin, he was one of a group of young upcoming writers; some of them became famous. Ngugi wa Thiong'o, James Ngugi at that time, was a classmate and friend. We expected much from Vyas. Wole Soyinka, who would win the Nobel Prize, had included Vyas in his anthology of African poets. I still have a copy, with two poems by "V. L.," signed to me by Vyas at a reading he gave to us in Meza.

"You are the real poet, Vyas," I said. "You always were . . ."

But what happened to you? Simply, exile and family. When the Asians were expelled from Uganda, Yasmin became stateless. The two of them went to Canada, and the rest of us followed from Tanzania, fearing that now anything could happen in the region.

"Yes, a good one," Yasmin said, "no matter what some editor says." She turned to me. "He sent three of his poems to a magazine for the first time. And got a rejection."

"He still writes poetry?"

"Yes."

"Yes," Vyas muttered. "He still does and he's pathetic . . . pathetic . . . pathetic."

The following spring Vyas was struck with gout and suffered terribly. Even in the winter he came out limping, wearing sandals and layers of socks. He turned vegetarian, which was how he'd been brought up, but took wine, and Sara, Yasmin, and I supplied him constantly with remedies and advice. When finally, after a year, he had recovered, he was still nervous about his food. Yasmin convinced him that he needed something extreme to clean up his system—he should go to Amarapur. Moez said why didn't they go together, and the two began to plan their trip, but the rest of us convinced them to go separately or they would argue all the time and return each with a heart attack or a stroke. The prospect of two corpses airlifted from India did not sound too far-fetched. When Vyas returned after a month at Amarapur, he was slim; his face looked firm and fresh, and I was reminded of the boy I had known back in Meza. The one I had my eye on, before Zool struck first.

"I wrote some poetry while there," he told me. "I'll publish it privately. Would you like a copy?"

"Of course I would!"

We were at a dinner at a Moroccan restaurant, the six of us. Zool and Moez were both away from the table.

"I still have that anthology you gave me," I told him with a smile. "*Poems from Black Africa.* Do you remember?"

"Soyinka? You do? Can I have it? I don't have a copy—with all that moving around we did."

"Well you can't have mine," I said. "It's signed."

To Anita, with love.

THE END OF THE WORLD

One day he was the strong, confident father and husband, protective; easy to laugh and just as easily sober or tender. They came to me for hugs and dug into my flesh, but if they had a problem it was to him they would turn. If it was politics or history, it was him not me. But soon after that fateful day—September 11, why be coy about it?—he became brooding, inward, sometimes paranoid, imagining threats and dire futures. Physically too he seemed older now, there had appeared the suggestion of a stoop, a shadow on his face. Had he always been dark, this scion of the Mughals, as he thought of himself?

That day on my way home from school I picked him up at a little past four, the hour he had said. As I cruised slowly into Sussex Avenue, he emerged, coming down the steps of Robarts Library with his backpack on him, grinning. It had been a good day of research and writing, apparently. Someone had given him an office to use on the fourteenth floor where he hardly saw anyone.

"Well? How was your day? Those brats wear you out?"

"You heard what happened—in New York?" I asked.

"No. What? Some shooting? Riots?"

I told him, and he said, "My God." He repeated it, an invocation to a being he always vehemently denied, and sat back. "No wonder all was quiet there inside . . . no one using the elevators . . ." He looked out his window, I at the traffic snarl ahead. And then he muttered, "Who will they go after to wreak their revenge . . . it's going to be terrible. Another war."

Prescient, but at the time I was startled by his response. Perhaps, now that I think about it, I was frightened too. For him, for us, and for the world. Like everyone else at the time I was in a state of shock. Something so unthinkable had happened, it felt as though the end of the world had just been announced. An alien force had landed on earth; an incurable disease was spreading rapidly across the globe; we could only wait.

I had watched the two buildings falling, crumbling, on television earlier that day at the school, along with the teachers and students who had rushed in a mob into the assembly hall. In a minute, the hall was jammed full, all of us staring in disbelief at the two screens above our heads. Watching a cataclysm—live, we were told, but the same clip was replayed over and over soundlessly like a silent prayer. The silence on the

TV screens, and all around me in the hall. Other than that, I don't recall anything else until I was in the car on my way to pick him up. This has not happened, I kept telling myself. It has not happened, an attack on New York. I have imagined it entirely; or I'll soon learn that it has been a hoax. Remember Orson Welles?

Later in the evening, when we had seen the twin towers collapsing at least three times with the kids, after they had gone up to their rooms, I looked at him questioningly. And he answered in an even tone, "That girl who was abducted, and her body found decomposed in High Park last month. Isn't that horrific? How many such murders happen every year?"

This was an act of war, I told him. It was symbolic. He agreed, symbolic because it was America that was attacked. Now there would be actual war. Rockets and bombs and tanks. More lives lost. Didn't I remember Vietnam?

"Don't you feel anything?—for the people who died today? For all that destruction?" I asked.

"Of course I do. But not more than I did for Rwanda. Or for Cambodia. Think of all the children murdered every year, even in America."

He showed no emotion at all at the dreadful sight we had just watched repeatedly on our television. His response was intellectual: one more mass act of violence. Surely thousands dying this morning an hour's flight away was closer than Rwanda ten years ago and Cambodia two decades before that?

I told him all this and more and left him alone before the empty television screen to mull by himself.

Upstairs, alone, I felt uneasy. An attack on New York. Buildings toppling. How many dead? Nothing could alter that. And yet that weight on the heart. A feeling, not articulate enough at the time, that I was a liar, a hypocrite. Only later I allowed myself the clarity to ask myself, how deep was that initial feeling, how genuine? I was a Canadian from a troubled part of the world, where millions lived in dire poverty; in my childhood our country had fought three wars, we had seen horrific violence in our streets. Memories of our subcontinent's Partition were recent. As many as a million people died at the time. My parents would mention the trainloads of corpses arriving at railway stations, people butchered while crossing the new borders between India and Pakistan. There had been losses in our own family that were never mentioned but still cast a long shadow. Was my response to the New York catastrophe too easy, too expected, and too pat, conditioned by my need to be like others, to belong? And for my children to belong?

In the following weeks the rhetoric everywhere was the same chorus of stock responses; and when the drumbeats of war sounded down south, I felt fortunate that we had chosen to come to a small and peaceful country.

More years ago than I care to count I watched Aslam at a student rally at the University in Karachi and fell instantly in love.

We were demonstrating against the war in Vietnam. I was only a naive freshman but I did not want to miss the thrill of doing something so daring. I was aware that this was an exciting period worldwide, and many people of our age were voicing opinions on the important issues of the day. We were the future. But I had grown up in the belief that communism was godless and despicable, and now here I was at a rally shouting support for the communists in Vietnam. We had stopped outside the entrance of the administration building, chanting our slogans, waiting to be addressed. "Out! Out! America out of Vietnam!" we chanted. Aslam stood on the steps facing us with two other senior students by his side, one of them a woman. He was impressive, not particularly handsome, but he had a certain charisma, with his wavy, ruffled hair tumbling down from his forehead, loose shirt with sleeves rolled partway, thin beard on his chin, and that fire in his eyes. I recall that his voice had become hoarse, I barely heard him in the noise, yet somehow he was still compelling. He raised a fist and we cheered. The woman beside him would periodically shout something in support; she had a thin voice, and was fair and small and delicate and wore pants and an oversized man's shirt. I could guess that he was having an affair with her. I imagine her clearly and her memory is a twinge that still remains.

From crumpled torn sheets in his hands Aslam read off messages of solidarity from student groups in Oxford, Paris, Frankfurt, New York, and Berkeley. There followed more cheering, then the rally broke up and the three speakers stood on the steps handing out sheaves of pamphlets to distribute. I walked up to Aslam to receive my share, and for a moment, when our eyes met, I was electrified. "Are you available later to discuss?" I managed, then breathlessly went on, "I'm not quite sure why we should support communists." "Oh? Sure, we can discuss that," he replied with a smile. "I'm sure I can convince you."

A few days later between morning classes I was sitting in the student canteen with my friends, having tea. The place was filled, everyone speaking at the top of their voice. The cacophony was a character of that place and always reminded me of birds inside a cage. There were four of us around a sticky, rickety table. One of the girls muttered something and I looked up startled to see Aslam Sheikh heading towards us in slow leisurely strides, his head tilted aside as though with a question. I took a deep breath and said to myself, So he's come. He stood at the opposite end of the table and looked at me.

"So, Rumi Lakhani, you wanted to know why we should support godless communists . . . Here I am at your service."

There was a hard smile on his face and a grit to his voice. His eyes, I noticed, were green. My friends stood up. One of them made a cheeky comment—"Yaar, this is too intellectual for us . . ."—and they vamoosed. As soon as they were gone Aslam sat down, then looked around and said, "Let's go outside where we can hear ourselves."

We crossed the road to the grass bank, where a few others had also come to seek refuge from the noise. We sat down on the ground, and he began.

"Now, the godless communists. Why should we be on their side?"

I mumbled something in response, and he said, "Don't worry. You are right, in a way. But we support what we think is the right cause, not one side or another. In the war in Vietnam we support the communists. We always support the oppressed people of the world. However, at the end of the day what we really support is always: Pakistan!"

"Pakistan! I'm so glad you said that . . ."

"Why? Didn't you think I was a good Pakistani?"

"No, it's not that, but . . ."

He laughed, and we chatted idly for a while. Too soon, a shadow fell on us and it was Asma, his companion from the rally, with a sweet smile. "Shall we go?" she asked him with a tilt of her head and a glance straight at me. She wore traditional attire that day, I remember in particular the bright pink, starched salwar. "Sure," he said, standing up and dusting himself. "Well, Rumi, see you around, then! Don't abandon the struggle!"

I felt foolish for my infatuation. But I avoided running across him then on. My friends teased me no end for a few weeks, reciting a famous forlorn line by the Urdu poet Ghalib—"it was not to be, our union"—to rile me. At the end of that year he graduated with his degree in journalism, and I didn't see him again until much later.

He came from a well-connected family of Lahore. Both his parents were lawyers, and his mother sometimes was in the news as an advocate for the rights of poor abused women. His older brother was on the Cricket Board and appeared in the news whenever the Pakistan national team was selected. Asma was the daughter of a general. And so they both were from our nation's elite and well-suited for each other. My family was of a modest background. Father worked as a post office bureaucrat, and Mother stayed at home. They had arrived in Karachi as a young refugee couple from Gujarat during the Partition and had a difficult time settling. We were the foreigners. Aslam's family were pukka Punjabis of the entitled sort, who had owned large tracts of Mughal-endowed land for generations. He would boast that their origins were in Kandahar, in Afghanistan, and his ancestors had come east to India with the army of Babur the Mughal. Sixteenth century.

After my graduation three years later, I took a job at a primary school in a wealthy neighbourhood. It was a pleasant job, but like most girls in my situation I was waiting to get married, though I also hoped to do a master's degree eventually. Aslam had become a pleasant memory, jogged whenever I saw—and read—his fiery or acerbic column in the progressive daily *Dawn*. Marriage proposals duly came, but wherever I showed interest, there was the condition that I not work. Marriage seasons followed one after another, and my parents were getting desperate. One day a pupil in my class was brought to school by both her mother and her uncle, who—to my great surprise—happened to be Aslam. I can only imagine how red I must have turned; he looked unruffled, of course, but we greeted each other warmly and agreed to meet later for coffee.

There was a café down the road from the school where we met. It was just past four p.m. He said he had travelled, to Norway and East Germany, but not been up to much else. I asked him about Asma. "Ah," he said, a little embarrassed. "You remember her. That would never have worked. We were too much alike."

We continued to meet at the café, usually every Thursday. After a few times he began to drop me home in his little Fiat, and later still we went out Saturday afternoons, when he would come to pick me up. My parents liked him, though they would have preferred someone more of our sort. But they insisted I should get married and Aslam agreed.

In my extended new family, I was the dark Gujarati, little better than a "Madrasi." I was always aware of this, you have to be, when fair skin is the chief measure of a woman's beauty. I could sense an anxiety in the women that my children would come out short, dark, and round-faced and bring shame to the family. More than once I heard the comment "What kind of name is Lakhani?—sounds Hindu . . ." Noses in the air. They were the fair Mughals, descendants of conquerors; we were the dark "converts" and exiles. And they were all thin and beautiful, the wives of influential Pakistani army people and politicians, educated in exclusive convent schools where they learned to play tennis and squash, and in our gatherings would often break off into exuberant northern Punjabi, so that I felt excluded. Our families hardly spent time together. And so when Aslam received a scholarship to spend a year, and possibly two years, in Michigan, I could hardly contain my excitement. I suppressed the urge to shout, "Yes, let's go!" and let him make the decision. The offer was a huge surprise. "Why would they give you a scholarship when you have demonstrated and railed against them?" I asked him. "Are you sure it's not a mistake?" He grinned. "They hope to seduce me to their side. Soft power. But they'll see, this fool is not so easy to seduce—except by his wife." The scholarship meant leaving his friends and the troubled country that he loved for two years, and that made him sad. But he was also happy to go to America. Who wasn't?

I would now have him all to myself. My feelings were selfish, but as my mother advised me, part of a woman's job is to wean her husband away from his family and friends. She, for her part, had already given me away at my marriage.

There were occasional student demonstrations on the Ann Arbor campus, for some cause or another having to do with racism, and Aslam naturally couldn't resist the action. I had to warn him, "Don't forget we are only guests here, Aslam." To which he would say, "Don't you understand, Rumi, in America you are free to express yourself. There are all kinds of opinions here." When I smiled at this, thinking, So America's not so bad, he added, "Even if at the end of the day it doesn't make a rat's arse of a difference." We spoke in Urdu, always, but he had a way of incorporating into it new expressions he had learned. It seemed that he adapted more to American ways than I did.

Towards the end of two years, his scholarship was running out. One day we learned that a couple from India who had become our friends and were in similar circumstances to us were leaving for Canada as immigrants. "Why don't we apply and see what happens? We don't have to go there, but let's give ourselves a choice!" I said. Aslam agreed, just to make me happy. And was trapped.

Fairly quickly we found work in Toronto from which to make a start, he as a freelance journalist, then a copy editor, I as a sessional teacher of English as a Second Language. We were modestly comfortable, reasonably happy, living in rental accommodation first in Bloor West then Don Mills. Something remained missing, however: the clamour of children. Echoes from my school in Karachi were a memory that kept pulling at me, while our folks missed no chance to send us reminders. But to my every hint or suggestion, the idealist would say he was not keen to bring more of "them" into a troubled, overpopulated world. Finally, when I found a permanent job and we became more secure and older and the evenings began to seem a little empty, he relented. Why not? We'll make good parents. Tariq was born. Overnight he changed, became the doting, anxious father. Two years later came Zahra. Aslam had brought his politics with him, but apart from a few demos, once when the Ku Klux Klan marched through Little India, activism simply amounted to having opinions and following world news, which he devoured. There remained some hope that we might return to Pakistan, both our families begging us to do so. Jobs awaited us, we were assured. We had stayed away too long. Our parents thirsted (their word) to see the grandchildren. But time passed, the children grew older and started school, and back there fundamentalism was on the rise; we knew we would not be going home to stay.

Toronto was gently liberal. The NDP, our party, was moderately left and during elections we allowed them to put up their signs on our lawn. You could say that now I had truly tamed the tiger, defanged the fiery old radical and turned him into a family man. Carrying bags of groceries, shoveling snow in winter, or sitting on the stairs struggling to put a snowsuit on Tariq, he was hardly the charismatic radical I had fallen in love with. But love and attraction evolve too, don't they? He was a happy father, he would make any sacrifice for his kids.

Then came that fateful day when two tall iconic buildings in New York collapsed like blocks of melting ice cream.

War was threatened, and we joined the protests. Saturday mornings we packed our lunches and took the subway downtown to go and march with a few thousand others on University Avenue in front of the American consulate. We were under no illusions. This demo lacked the noise and electricity, the conviction of our youth marches, missing was the expectation—the belief—that we could make a difference. Today's youth had mostly stayed away; we ourselves were older, subdued and orderly. Quite without hope. But protest we must, we felt, against a needless war.

There were bombings in Karachi and Lahore, where our families lived. And in London, Bali, and Delhi. Nowhere seemed safe. But then why didn't we come out against these acts of terror, Zahra asked one evening at our dinner table congress. She confessed that in her history class she had boasted that on Saturdays her parents joined the protests against war in Iraq. Her teacher had queried, "Are you a Muslim?" and all eyes turned to fix on Zahra. The teacher followed with the other question, Why didn't Muslims protest against Islamic terrorism? Yes, yes, echoed her classmates. Why didn't they? I had been asked this question too, by my own pupils, and Aslam had seen it in a newspaper column. We looked at each other. We had no answer. There could be no answer. What is Islamic about an act of terror? How do you protest against terrorism? Do terrorists have a local embassy, do they listen to opinions? We commiserate with friends and neighbours, with anyone we can. With ordinary people, like you and I, who could have been the victims. Does it have to be repeated all the time that Islam is a religious faith, it's not genetic? How does my family bear responsibility for 9/11? Do we now have to wear a badge declaring our origins, swear our loyalty and innocence, deny affiliation with any criminal calling himself a Muslim?

It had come to seem that the more real and constant fear we lived under was not of a bomb on a train but of being thought of as people who might plant one. Or tacitly support the murderers who did. Our safe world, our complacent life "in the best country in the world" had been shattered. We did not know who we were anymore. Everything was wrong about us: where we came from, the way we looked, our names. We had proudly called ourselves Canadians, with a background. Everyone has a background. But now we were Muslims first, to others and to ourselves. Terrorism was ours, a disease we had brought with us. We felt ashamed, afraid to say the wrong thing or be misunderstood. We found ourselves speaking quietly and casting furtive glances whenever we discussed politics, even Canadian politics. We warned the kids to behave. What do you tell a girl who thinks one of her teachers consistently gives her the suspicious eye? Or a boy who is taunted with calls of "Osama"? The terror was in us now.

"Extremism is dangerous. It should be opposed," I said to him, as though he promoted it. "We've always believed that. Terrorism is murder."

"Of course. It's murder, nothing else."

Formulas, mantras that must be repeated over and over for the sake of the kids, who were now upstairs, ears peeled as always for discussions downstairs.

In Madrid that morning a train had been bombed.

In the brief silence that fell between us we eyed each other, much remaining unsaid. This was no time for nuances, to point out that many more innocent people had already died in the attack on Iraq than at the World Trade Center, that the entire country faced destruction, that even in the United States innocent people were being tortured or taken away merely on suspicion, without trials. We had already quietly stopped going to the protests. It was as though we didn't trust our own kids to be sensible and know the limits of dissent, and we had to mislead or lie to them. Suddenly we would drop our voices, or talk loudly when we wished them to hear something edifying.

I said, now dropping my voice, "We must keep telling them the same thing. Terrorism is murder. Violence cannot be justified. We live in a safe and democratic country. And remember, don't talk politics when they are around."

"I know. But they are not stupid—thank God. They can see what's going on in the world. They will form their own opinions."

And they can read our faces. They'll see anxiety and bitterness. And they are brown, their names are Muslim. How do we cope with that?

They knew about their father's radical student days in Karachi. He had boasted about his activism, at a time when it was all right to do so. He told them how he had come out in support of minorities in Pakistan and against its army's atrocities in Bangladesh, against apartheid in South Africa, British policies on Rhodesia, and America's war in Vietnam. In Toronto he had marched against the Ku Klux Klan. I was there too, I told them, though not as loudly. Neither of us had wanted them to grow up complacent, disengaged from the world. Now we both desired to erase those pictures of protest from their minds, my husband more than I. A panicky father.

"Terrorists are criminals," out of the blue he would announce solemnly to Tarik with a nod. "Remember that." They were envious of our freedoms and privileges. They were psychopaths. Islam possessed backward and dangerous ideas. Remember that.

Was this the radical I had married? The intellectual who worshipped Noam Chomsky, Frantz Fanon, and Che Guevara? Previously he would have analyzed the issues, spoken of state and radical terrorism, terms that he himself taught me; he would have brought up the example of the Sufis, who practiced mystical and joyful forms of Islam that embraced all faiths. He was well read. He knew nuance. But he abandoned it all for fear that his kids, his son, Tariq, especially, might turn brash and radical—and then what? Trapped in a sting operation by the authorities into attempting something stupid. Arrested and tortured.

"I don't want Tariq doing something silly . . . even saying something can land him in—"

"Guantanamo? You're the one being silly . . ."

But Tariq, sensing his anxiety, had learned to bait him. He was at that age. At the dinner table he would come up with arguments that would have alarmed me if I didn't know my son better. But Aslam readily took the bait and spluttered and argued and raged, and the two would be at each other.

"What does it matter?" Zahra would get up from the table, exasperated. "You two stop it! We live in Canada, look outside for a moment. That world is far away." She would storm out.

Aslam became depressive. He put on weight and his blood pressure shot up. He stopped going to the gym, seeing accusing eyes everywhere. His squash partner Bendtner was, he told me privately, "Bush and Rumsfeld combined."

I warned Tariq not to provoke his father.

"I only wanted an honest discussion with him, see what he thought."

"There are better ways to do it."

"Well, I'm not going to become a terrorist, if that's what you think."

"You should still be careful of what you say. Especially in school, or to your friends. We live in a time of war."

"And we are the wrong colour and religion."

I gave him a look and ruffled his hair. That was a fine one coming from him. Like his father, he didn't believe in any faith.

He pulled himself away from me with a smile. We had been a happy family, close to each other, cultured and educated, who enjoyed talking and debating issues. What had happened to us?

Gradually things became calmer, and we learned to cope with the world better. Obama came and brought hope. The war moved to Afghanistan and continued but seemed distant to us in Toronto. Acts of terrorism elsewhere alarmed us but not to disrupt our lives. Once, when we drove to Ann Arbor to see some friends, Aslam with his fierce look and his surname Sheikh hardly raised an eyebrow at Immigration but I was thoroughly questioned. We laughed and I got teased. It was how the world was and we were getting used to it. The extra scrutiny became the norm. Tariq quietened down but would fish out Aslam's past issues of leftist magazines that he'd kept out of sight. "He's smart," Aslam said to me with approval. He had learned to trust the kids. Among ourselves we discussed Karachi and the violence in the streets there. I was planning to visit my parents, who said there was nothing wrong with Karachi, to which Aslam replied, "Everything is wrong with it," but agreed I should go.

One Friday evening we returned home from seeing a play and, taking off our boots and coats, came into the living room, happy to see the kids. They were sitting quietly on the carpet watching a movie. But there was something wrong with the scene that momentarily made it seem like we were in the wrong house, and I gave a start. Zahra wore a scarf over her head. Not an ordinary scarf but a tight, blue hijab.

I gave a quick look at Aslam and put a finger to my lips.

"Well, well, new look!" I said in reply to Zahra's challenging look. Tariq had an amused smile, and Aslam a rather lame one.

We had dinner, and later I went up to Zahra's room to question her. She was sitting up in her bed, a textbook in her lap, obviously waiting for me to arrive.

"What's with this thing?"

"What thing?"

"You know, this cloth on your head."

"It's called a hijab. I'm simply asserting my identity."

"And what's that?"

"My Muslim identity."

"Well, I am a Muslim, you never saw me wearing that!"

"Maybe you were scared to."

"I never wore it. When I was young we wore a loose dupatta, which fell to the shoulder anyway."

She turned and gave me a long look, with those large brown eyes of hers, now accentuated by her head cover. She did look pretty.

"Have you thought how you would answer Allah, when your time comes?" she asked me quietly.

I took a deep breath. My heart was pounding. "I can deal with Allah. Let's talk about this later, just you and I. Meanwhile come for dessert downstairs. We've brought back a nice chocolate cake."

She got up and followed me. Tariq joined us on the landing.

At the table the three of us waited for Aslam to come down. When he did, he had changed into sweatpants and T-shirt and wore a strained smile.

"You're waiting. Sorry," he said. As he sat down he saw Zahra's defying eyes on him. His approval, or disapproval, was what mattered most to her. He said, "Darling—you can wear anything you like. If it's decent."

THE SENSE OF AN ENDING

When do you know it's finally over? When he drapes his arm around you in bed and it feels like a log, and his body feels like a weight against you. But it's you that's turned cold, and you ache inside because you cannot revive that old feeling of warm security and contentment when he enveloped you, and you wonder. You want to ask how or why but you know it happens, and reasons don't matter. The same way your once close brother and only sibling is now a perfect stranger, and your best friend in school speaks to you formally in English whenever you meet, which is not often.

She lifts up his hand and transports it slowly across her body and drops it gently back to his side. He's not sleeping yet, probably asking himself these same questions.

That first time he held her from behind, they were standing at the door of her apartment. I always wanted to do that, he murmured, putting his hands inside her blouse and cupping both her breasts. She could feel him harden against her and responded ever so slightly with a jiggle. That was early days and he approached her with caution. They had declared their undying commitment to each other, and everything looked wonderful for the future.

Familiarity, they say. But that's bullshit. On the contrary, there are times when she does feel an ache, a prick of emotion, the longing for that old love to return. It has to be there when you've spent all these years together. The happy and the sad moments and the obstacles overcome in the joint resumé of the marriage. But then one day life's handed you a new pair of glasses, saying, Look, and you see those quirks and flaws in all their clarity that were once barely noticeable, you see the sharper face lines and the softer flesh, the slower movements and the thinning hair, the set ways that irritate, until little remains of that magic . . . when you waited anxiously, longed to see the familiar calm face again when he had been away for a conference. They had begun together in a spirit of adventure, having relished their single lives after college and now learning partnership. It was like going to a new country, like when she first left Dar for America, and everything was exciting. Nobody tells you about the anxiety of having children; how that frantic preoccupation eats your years away silently like acid, the time spent on schools and activities, in sheer worrying and doubting, and the money spent, because we wanted nothing but the best for them. Private schools, music lessons, sports camps. And finally, the boys are doing well. And we are spent.

There was no passion to begin with. She repeats the diagnosis, which has come to her only recently, she almost whispers the words aloud, her lips ungluing for a second, and she edges away from the clinging warmth of his body aura as if repulsed. There was no passion. You read about it in those schoolgirl romances that came from England and saw it in the movies. She never experienced it, even to be thwarted in it. There was no sweet ache to nurse in the dark nights. She had waited vainly for that right, that perfect person to appear whom she desired beyond anything else; who consumed her soul. But this one came along in time and wanted her and she told herself not to be foolish. Life was not a night at the movies. He was the safe alternative, a bird in hand; a university professor, tall and fair, and not a bad face but for the beaky nose. Decent. Do you want a husband and family or not? Theirs was a cultivated love. Stable, mature, thoughtful, and almost arranged. An agreement to love. An option.

It was American Thanksgiving, and she had come for her dutiful visit from DC to see her mother in Toronto. Her mother had hinted on the phone that she had a nice surprise waiting for her. Nadia could guess. "What surprise is she talking of?" she asked her brother nevertheless when she gave him her arrival time. "You know," he said. A boy, that's what her mother said at the breakfast table when Nadia arrived, and he was a find. She had better get serious. There were girls lining up for him. Good family, good-looking, a prestigious job. It had been her father's dear wish, he would find his eternal peace, his *asal-me-wasal*, only when she got married and settled down. The usual blackmail. Her father, who was healthy by all counts and took long walks every day, had collapsed with a heart attack a year ago, and her mother with her long list of ailments pined on, saying all the time, "I wish He would take me now. But even He's waiting for our Nadia to marry."

The next day, Azim had driven them to an apartment in Don Mills, where many Dar immigrants had come to stay. A frail-looking woman in a long dress, with almost translucent pale features, welcomed them with a smile; she was Sheru Bai, obviously the prospect's mother. There was another woman present, Nuru Bai, her sister, and a younger woman, Parin, her daughter, visiting from Michigan where she was doing a Ph.D. And then there was he, looming uncomfortably behind the three women, the background but the important business.

Nadia recognized Amyn immediately as one of the academic stars of their generation back in their small universe in East Africa. Back then everybody knew about the supersmart boys, how they would go on to make their mark in the world. But the world changed and here they all were in North America. Amyn taught English literature at Trinity College. Nadia got along well with him from the moment they were introduced, and they happened to sit next to each other, first in the living room, where the families briefly gathered and introduced themselves, and later at the dining table. They found that they could talk, they had common interests in books and music and tennis. Both had attended university in the States. And they must have crossed paths at Dar's new public library, with its spacious study hall and all those new English novels, where it turned out they had both gone to study for their final school certificate exams. They might even have borrowed the same books from there. A connection.

A generous spread had been laid out for the guests. Enough to dull her brain, she thought in good humour. The chai was exquisite though sweet. Nothing was said about the marriage proposal, it was as if this were a routine invitation, though there hung an air of formality and good behaviour over the proceedings. As they departed, Sheru Bai said to Nadia's mother, "Please be a little quick." With your decision, was what she meant. *Jara jaldi karja.* Obviously there were others waiting to grab this choice suitor.

That same evening Amyn called and asked if he could take her out for dinner the next day. She couldn't, Nadia said, she had reserved her evenings for her mother. They settled on lunch at the Faculty Club. They met at the entrance and shook hands. Inside, he paused to sign her in before they found a table. A civilized place, she thought to herself, looking around at the oak fittings, the glowing chandeliers and antique wall sconces. A middle-aged waiter with a Scottish accent and patronizing manner brought them the menu. They both ordered the spinach soup and salmon, which were the specials, and a glass of white. And they chatted as comfortably as they had done before.

Over coffee Amyn brought up the subject.

"I don't want to rush you or anything, Nadia. I know a proposal has been made . . . for . . . you know what, but I think I would like to speak for myself. You've been ambushed, I know. But I really like you. We do have a lot in common and I think we can make a go of it . . ." They both laughed and he added, "And make a success of it. I see myself . . . loving you." He blushed.

"Well," she said. "That's a mouthful."

"Yes."

"Give me a little time . . . a day or two."

"Of course."

He walked her to her car, parked on St. George Street, where she discovered she had received a ticket.

"Let me pay for it," he said, grabbing it. "I invited you here."

They said goodbye and he gave her a peck, and he closed the door when she had sat down and saw her drive off.

She liked him, of course. How could she not? He seemed just right. Not someone to sweep you off your feet, but then what did that mean? He was comfortable. She would grow to love him. After all, what were the prospects for meaningful relationships in DC? A few Europeans at the Bank, and an

Egyptian at the Fund. Nice men, sophisticated and exotic, but at the end of the day, alien and transient.

She let a day pass and called him Sunday afternoon.

"Yes," she said past the first greeting.

"Yes?"

"Yes," she laughed at the raised pitch in his voice.

He couldn't contain himself. "Ever since I met you I have been praying to whatever is out there, Shiva, Krishna, Allah, Jesus and Mary . . . for just this one wish of mine to come true. It will be wonderful, I promise you. Our love will grow . . ."

They went for a late coffee, had cognac to follow, and made plans for the future. She would move to Toronto and find a job. She liked Toronto. Yes, she wanted kids.

It was nice. Sweet. Ups and downs, of course, but a predictable journey. Was it worth giving up a cushy job in DC for a lesser one, losing touch with friends, the nights out at the Folger or the Kennedy Center, the train to New York? But in my new life I wasn't lonely, had someone I could speak to in Kutchi, indulge in nostalgia and recall the life we had left behind. We made new friends together. Became lovers. Now the boys are gone, returning only for Christmas, and there are only the faults and flaws to glare at. His slippers are never aligned, the drawers are left ajar, as though somewhere deep inside he is afraid of closure. Does it matter? It doesn't. Then why do these habits glare at you like cracks in a wall? Why do his changing looks embarrass you when you know you're not as supple as you once were? It's because of the emptiness that's come to occupy me.

The next morning he's made coffee and is ready to go when she comes down. He watches her. Always trim, still pretty. He can't help a glow of pride that he won her. Not quite PC, some of his students would pounce on him if they heard him speak those words. Won her. He knows that his friends still wonder, How did the bugger manage to snare her? He gives her a kiss on the cheek.

"I've been thinking," she says.

He smiles, he's waiting.

"I thought I'd go visit Layla in DC."

"The one from—"

"Nairobi, yes. She lived with a guy from Ghana for a while. They broke up. Now she's alone and she's invited me. Do you mind?"

"Of course not. You should go, if you feel like it. But I didn't know you were in touch, or were still close."

"Well, recently. When she became single again."

"Go. You'll feel good. You don't want me to come with you?" He waits then gives her another peck. "Only kidding. You should know that."

She looks relieved.

All those years, he says to himself, walking to the station. It was like working on a long project together. Bringing up the boys. Hard work but fulfilling. Gave you a purpose, and they bound you together. With kids there's always something to do or say, and it's worthwhile, you'll do anything for them, even waking up at dawn for band or hockey. The medical emergencies. The few times he would rather forget. Still, he would have preferred a third child, a girl. But two is enough, she said, and three would be stretching our means. True enough, if you want to send them all to Upper Canada or Branksome Hall.

Before he enters the station he texts brief *hi*'s to the boys. *How you doing? Fine*, Irfan replies instantly. One word, but good enough.

That sudden announcement, I thought I'd go to DC. It felt like a stab, but why? It just did. An announcement or a notice? Is there a difference? Washington is her past, why call upon it now? She and Layla had spent a lot of time together way back. Nadia was at the World Bank, Layla at the IMF—the Fund, as they called it. Great jobs, and Nadia had given hers up for the sake of their marriage and come to Toronto. What did she leave behind? He's never inquired about the details, what do they matter? And he? She never inquired either.

He comes out on St. George Street and reads a message from their younger son, Arman. It's longer, as always. *Yay, I got my visa for India! Doing great! And you?* He smiles, already feeling better.

His day is typical. At ten he teaches his African Lit class. They discuss the question Why did Achebe dislike Conrad?

An animated discussion, rather neatly divided along racial lines, most of the white kids standing up for Conrad, in which Amyn takes no definite position. He's there to prompt and suggest, to teach them how to analyze, without himself getting personally involved. Two students take him up on that. But you must believe something, Prof! Don't you stand for anything? He does not take the bait. Not for this class, he replies, I don't. But it's not the first time the point of his reticence has come up in a class. He can't help it, for every argument he sees a counter. He's been accused of hiding behind fairness and literary jargon in order to remain safe. After the class, for about an hour in his office he looks at a few of the applications for next year's college admissions and makes notes for his short list. At twelve he meets his colleague Appa for lunch to discuss their current project, a conference. The arts councils have refused assistance, but the Dean has come to their rescue, scrounging up a small sum from a reserve fund. There's a caveat: he's asked them to involve local communities. The university has to reach out. That's easy to say, but how do you do that? Use a student, Appa suggests, he has one in mind, a Tamil. Involve two of them, Amyn says. He has an Ismaili in his class. After lunch he goes back to his office, looks at his mail, and reads more applications. At four he attends a history seminar at the Munk Centre next door, after which he leaves for home.

How did he end up in this profession? He'd been an economics major at Penn. But encouraged in an elective literature class, he took a minor in English, and at a whim studied for a higher degree in the subject. He had a gift for it, his supervisors said. And miraculously he was offered a job for which a couple of dozen had been turned away. All he had to do was come to Toronto and say his piece in a seminar. He had not even submitted his thesis formally. It had been too easy, and at heart he was never satisfied. He had been shown a cocoon and moved right into it. Tucked away in his office at the college or his study at home with his books, dissecting stories and poems according to the theories of the day, a post-colonialist, a post-modernist, a deconstructionist, using jargon to spin theories like jalebis, as someone derisively put it. Or webs, to veil realities, as he himself sometimes despaired. He should have written stories or poetry to express himself, dug into his soul. Produced art, not argument. He's become a passionless scholar instead. Our meddling intellect / Mis-shapes the beauteous forms of things / We murder to dissect. Wordsworth.

It's too late to change careers now. But Nadia was impressed initially that she'd married a professor. He was a pundit, a learned man who could quote poets. That meant something back there, long ago. The illusion was gone in no time.

Layla picks her up at Dulles. Dark and lithe, softer now but still sensuous in a clinging white dress; the broad smile, the lips thickened with purple lipstick, perhaps give the game away. Nadia's disappointed but decides not to be. We have all aged. But DC looks the same, if you don't pay close attention to the clothes.

First thing, they lunch at a French restaurant in Georgetown, as they did in the past, once a month or so at la coquette, which of course is no longer there. Nadia catches up with news about people she had known here. Karla the British girl married a Kenyan and went to Nairobi; Josephine returned with Bruce to Paris, now is back in DC by herself. Still at the Bank. Arvind married a woman from Bombay, settled down, has two kids and has grown fat; a celebrity now, riding high on the success of his book on the 2008 market crash. Pulitzer. Bestseller. And hardly to be seen, Layla thinks it's the Indian wife. Nadia once had eyes on him. She has to struggle to recall the others from the hazy collective they've become in her memory. They partied together, played tennis and bridge, went for brunches and concerts. Nadia's Wimbledon brunch was the event of the year every July, kicking off with champagne and strawberries, what else, and then a lavish spread to follow. Croissants and bagels, sausages and kippers, cheeses. A crowded, boisterous event, the men's final followed sporadically during the replays, and the American brat John McEnroe the rage. It was a charmed life, though stirred with that essential and irrevocable loneliness of the exile.

"And you? . . . Any men?" Nadia asks.

"A few . . ."

"And?"

"Nothing that lasted. What about you? What's married life like? You and your husband seem to have steered a steady ship. I met him only once, that time at the wedding. A solid person." She pauses, then blurts out, "You can't be happy with him . . . all those years? Nadia, of all people?"

Always blunt. And subversive. Nadia gives a smile. "Could have been worse," she says.

"That's hardly a recommendation for married life."

She refuses the challenge. But is that what she wanted to say, Could have been worse? And solid? Yes, she could write an essay on solid character.

That evening they go for dinner at a jazz club, flirt with a group of young political types, laugh and giggle a lot, then continue drinking at home, still catching up on the past. The following day at noon they drive to Bretton Woods to play tennis. Nadia's partner is Soren, tall and charming, mature, an excellent player but patient with her game, which to her grief is almost gone after long neglect. Layla convinced Arvind to come and he's her partner while his wife watches. They play a laborious set, after which they sit down for a light lunch. But Nadia and Soren have hit it off and he takes her out in his Maserati for an afternoon tea that ends with champagne. Nadia has the feeling that all this was planned. She doesn't mind. Soren is a consultant with the Bank, advising on a project in Mozambique to rebuild villages that were destroyed during the civil wars. He's just returned from

Maputo. Previously he was in Vietnam. Upper-class French despite the name, his manners are what you would expect. How she's missed such charm, such class, she admits to herself. They exchange contact information and agree to play singles the following afternoon. Can he take her out for dinner afterwards? Of course he can.

What is she doing?

The second time at tennis she is not as bad. He doesn't take her out but cooks for her at his home, an old house in Georgetown furnished as you would expect for a single man like him. He is an accomplished chef. The asparagus is from his garden, and so are the herbs; the ginger is from Vietnam, the pepper from Szechuan, and the lamb from a farm in Virginia. The Burgundy he opens is exquisite, from an estate in France that he knows well. I'd forgotten that wine could be such an experience, she thinks.

They talk about themselves, reveal details. There is a studied deliberation to Soren's manner in contrast to his agility on the court. But the grace carries over from tennis to intimate dinner. "I am rather ordinary," he says. With a smile, a twinkle. She laughs. "Tell me more."

He was born in a village in Argonne and after a degree in economics from the Sorbonne he went for his graduate work to Harvard. His first marriage to a Dane had not worked out, and he is—shall we say, cautious now.

"And you? Who is this charming, beautiful woman who's

descended from the cold north suddenly? And sits, unbelievably, in front of me?"

"More ordinary than you are."

She was born in Dar es Salaam, Tanzania, she says. Her father was a partner in an electric shop. She went to high school there, then to college at Oberlin, and soon after found a job at the World Bank. It was hiring Africans. She tells him how she met Layla, how she got married and moved to Toronto. Two sons.

It turns out he has a daughter in Geneva, married.

They have dinner, more wine. He offers her his best cognac, of which she takes a sip. It is a heady evening, on the edge of possibility.

She's arranged to have coffee and dessert with Layla and some acquaintances from her Tanzanian past. She cannot get out of it, and reluctantly they part. It's eleven when Soren calls her a cab. As he says goodbye, his embrace lingers, his body tightens, he squeezes her hand.

She arrives at a modest apartment on M Street, where they're already waiting for her. Her cousin Salim has come from Silver Spring. She last saw him five years ago in Toronto. It turns out to be a fun and raucous evening, and she meets people she's not seen in ages.

Back at Layla's house, as Nadia undresses in her room, Layla calls her over. She's sitting on her bed, leaning against the headboard, legs stretched out, a magazine open idly on her lap. "Come, sit. Let's talk," she says and makes way. Smiling.

She's put on a selection of sentimental old Indian film songs that remind them of their schooldays, all about heartbreak. As they would do in the past, they take turns translating the key lines—*Simple heart, what's happened to you? Giver of my life, I've lost faith in your world; If there were no grief, who would pen songs?*—and laugh and let the tears flow in turns, without inhibition. At some point Nadia gives an audible, uncontrolled sob from the throat and turns away.

"What's it, my dear?"

Nadia shakes her head.

"What is it, tell me, Nadia. Shed it off. Come on."

"It's all been wasted, my life. I've so missed something . . ."

"Something what? Tell me."

Nadia waits, then:

"I feel that I've never loved, really loved. Never got the chance. And now it's almost over, my life . . ."

She wipes her eyes.

"Nonsense. It's not over. It's midlife . . . Are you sick? Is there something you've not told me?"

Nadia shakes her head.

"Look at you—you're still good-looking. Your husband loves you?"

"Amyn . . . yes. I think so."

"So what? Chuck him. Take your life back."

"How can I? After all these years?"

"Dump him."

Nadia is in tears again, and Layla pulls her over to comfort her. She murmurs, "Did Soren . . . propose?"

"I think so."

"Say yes. Have a last glorious hurrah, show a finger to life before it's too late. He'll sweep you off your feet. Besides, he's a nice man, from an ancient family. This can actually lead somewhere. I'm jealous."

"Really?"

Layla starts to cry, and they fall asleep in each other's arms as dawn breaks outside.

The next morning an aroma of coffee wafts upstairs. Layla, hearing her, shouts, "Coffee is ready! And croissants!" Nadia sits on her bed, stares with a smile at Soren's card. On the blank side he's written a brief message, "Lovely to meet you! I would like to stay in touch . . . Possible?" in an exquisite hand. She recalls that extra squeeze when they said goodbye, that exchange of looks, the anticipation. She lets the card drop into the trash basket.

Amyn returns home and has leftover curry for dinner. She'd frozen it for him the day before. Curry the next day always tastes better. That's an old adage and it's true. It's Friday and she's gone, having texted him earlier that she found a flight to DC that she could take today instead of Saturday. His first instinct upon entering the empty house was to give her a call, but he resisted. She should have her time. He's jealous, of course. With the boys gone, they're as free as a young couple now, and there's a lot they could do together but they lack the will. That inertia—all the karma of a marriage weighing them down. It seems she couldn't wait to get away. And Layla is pure mischief, he recalls. He reads a new book by a young author from Togo he likes, makes notes in the margins while listening to music. Then he listlessly turns his laptop on and checks his emails. Casually—so he thinks—he Googles a name. And there it is. Nilufer Somani. Nilu.

After what, thirty-three years? Still pretty, he thinks, staring hard at the three-quarter-length photo on the screen. In a business suit now, hair short as before but styled. Perhaps dyed. What would he say to her? I survived, Nilu.

He had gone to Cambridge, Mass, from Ithaca, New York, and stayed at his friend Adil's, where he met Nilu at a dinner. One of those expatriate gatherings in a student house, she from the Congo and speaking French too. All of them new graduates in their twenties, from "back there" and not more than a few years in the US, scattered across the northeast, excited to be where they were and doing what they did. Linked by Amtrak, they met regularly in their different cities. This time someone new was present, discovered by Adil in Cambridge, and Amyn was sitting beside her on the floor and they got into a passionate discussion—about Kierkegaard, he remembers that—while the rest were on about Nixon and the Watergate hearings that had preoccupied the entire nation. He had never felt such a connection to anyone before, never met anyone so empathetic, with interests so close to his. Even as they talked, he trembled, staring into her eyes, thinking, this is surely it. Back in Ithaca he would call her often, and they had long conversations that became progressively intimate.

Two months later she invited him to Cambridge, and he stayed again with Adil. Having arrived Friday evening, he agreed to meet her for coffee Saturday morning at a place called the Blue Parrot. When they met, he was surprised to find her edgy and in a hurry. She had to go soon. This was to be their rendezvous, what happened? "Wait, what's the hurry? I want to tell you something," he insisted. She blushed. "Me too," she said softly. "But later." He had imagined that the two of them would go out for dinner, but instead she invited him and Adil to a dinner with her friends that evening. They met at a Chinese restaurant called Mayflower. She had come with five other people, and there was a guy with her, a Pakistani businessman their age from New York, wearing smart clothes that stood out, brash and offensive, everything Amyn could never be. Would never want to be. His name was Nawaz and he sat next to Nilu, his arm wrapped possessively behind her chair, with an air of triumph directed at Amyn across the table.

She never met his accusing eye. But she had crucified him, before a pitying gallery. His fortune cookie said something like, If you fail try and try again. He read it out and everyone laughed. It took him months to recover. Where had he gone wrong to let her slip away? A letter arrived saying she had gotten engaged. And he replied with a soppy one, the thought of which still embarrasses him, saying he would always be her friend. Friend! He heard of her wedding that same year from her sister, and later that she had moved to California. Where, he sees, she's now an estate agent in San Jose. Selling dreams. Why the maiden name? Had that married surname proved too burdensome in the end? Or the man? She did not belong with that sort, not the girl who read Kierkegaard and was so concerned about the world. He smiles. She made the right choice: safety. Finger poised: should he contact her? No.

The next morning he watches English soccer on television. Nadia doesn't care about watching sports, but Amyn always excuses himself Saturday mornings, saying that after a week of books and papers he deserves this escape. At half-time, disappointed for his team, he picks up his iPad and is stunned by a flurry of emails with the news that Professor Appadurai, "Appa," had suddenly collapsed in a restaurant the previous night and died. He was sixty.

Amyn had known Appa for thirty years, ever since Appa arrived from Vancouver to take up a job at Trinity, two years after Amyn. Appa was from Sri Lanka. The two of them had sat in meetings, taught classes together, organized seminars and conferences. Edited two books. They would disagree and argue, Appa with passion and Amyn calmly, but they always reached a compromise. And Appa would say, "You always do this to me, Amyn, I forget which side I was on!" But he had been reckless in stating his opinions and despite his popularity with students he had missed a promotion. He became bitter, took to railing against institutional racism. Amyn calls up Appa's wife, Anita, who's weeping, and gives her his condolences. The next afternoon he drives to a hall in High Park to view the body and embraces Anita, who's with her son and daughter and their partners. Appa looks handsome in a grey suit, as he always did for his classes. They've put a shine on his bald head. His published books are displayed in a glass case at the hall entrance. They include the two he edited with Amyn.

Monday morning Nadia calls and says she's arriving that afternoon.

"I'll pick you up. I have taken the day off," he tells her.

"No need to."

"I'll come. But . . ."

He tells her about Appa. She gasps, "Oh my God!" and there's a long silence between them.

"Funeral is this morning. I'm just off there, then I'll come and pick you up. The airport's close by."

"Okay. Are you all right?"

"Yes, I'm all right."

She did not miss him. But she realizes that he'd been there somehow in the shadow of their life together. She had appreciated that he had not called her, that he had left her alone.

He comes to bed late and lies on his back. Appa's death has hit him hard, she can tell, though he tries not to show it. They were not so very close, not as close as he is to some of his high school buddies in the city, but Appa was a constant factor in his life. Close in a special way. She can sense his breathing, just manages to hear a suppressed sigh. He does not move closer as he often does to put his arm around her. She turns to face him instead, and she stares at him.

WHAT YOU ARE

Zakia

I always believed I was African American. After all, who has doubts about what they are? True, my mom is Tanzanian Swahili, but Dad is true-blue Black American. With a capital B. I took pride in my early roots in America, not forgetting the heritage of Black oppression, and that many of our ancestors came as slaves, and that we resisted and fought back. Malcolm X and MLK, the Black Panthers. I've often recalled them and others as a young Black person growing up. And we've produced geniuses, given culture to the entire world. Music. Fashion. Idiom. A President whose image and accomplishments will live on when most of the others are forgotten.

Imagine my astonishment, my rage, my every negative feeling, the poison welling up inside me, when I discovered—was told blithely—just like that!—that in actual fact I was totally, absolutely one-hundred-percent Indian. A low-caste Indian woman, to boot, though caste means nothing to me because I am American first.

How do I cope with that? What do I do with myself now? I touch my skin, I scratch it with my nails, watch the red blood creeping out; I grab my hair; I look at my eyes up close. What am I? What *am* I?

"We thought the past had best be forgotten; it would only confuse you. You were ours, more than ours."

"How can I be more than yours, Mom, unless I am not yours in the first place?"

"That's not what I meant. You were ours and that was that. Why should it make a difference now?"

"Then why bring it up *now*?"

"We thought you were old enough . . . anyway, your dad . . ."

I turned to my dad. Big and looming, professorial, with his drawl and considered speech; until recently he smoked a pipe. He can quote pages of Baldwin and Langston Hughes. Sported an Afro once. Marched on Washington in Sixty-three. And I was no longer a part of that? Was excluded? He could probably read my thoughts; standing next to Mom, his hand on her shoulder, watching our exchange.

Mom stood up and brought in a tray of tea from the kitchen. She's one for tea. Ultra-sweet chai, with maandazi for breakfast, my favourite, the Swahili sweet fried pockets. Soft brown crust, hollow inside.

"That's right," he said. "We thought you were old enough… to know your other heritage."

"Which is what?"

"The Indian one, as Mom told you. Gujarat. That much I know."

"You must know more."

What is Gujarat, I don't want to be Gujarat. I am African American. I am Black, and proud, as he used to say when I was a kid.

For God's sake. I have a grandmother in Philadelphia, who loves me. I have cousins, one of whom plays basketball for Kentucky, another a nerd at Cornell.

My thoughts must have blazed out in garish neon in that silence. How could they not see them, they who introduced me, made me a part of a family? African American. We did not say more on the subject. I went up to my room to be alone. I tried to read, and look at some reports from my work, but how do you distract your mind from that one question, What am I now? Who am I? Has anything changed? Was there someone else in the world whom I had been stolen from? Bought from? Who loved me but had to let me go to rich America? Why? What would I have become, had I stayed back there, in Tanzania? I couldn't get the picture out of my head, a vague picture of a woman without a face but with a headscarf, sitting on the floor somewhere. Why on the floor? Search me. Would

I wear that sari thing or a hijab—like that woman, my real mother?

The father didn't even come to my mind.

The next morning I came down feeling like a zombie. I must have looked it. Mom came over and gave me a hug, which I reciprocated, but not enough, I think. Dad squeezed my arm.

"We have to talk," he drawled.

"I think I'll postpone my return—take the train tomorrow."

"That's a good idea. Breakfast first, then we go to the living room and talk. All right?"

He looked deep into my eyes. I nodded. "All right, Dad." How could he be anything else to me?

So this is my story. Martin Stewart, native of Philadelphia, arrived in Tanzania as a Peace Corps volunteer in 1967, a rare Black specimen—most of them tended to be whites—sporting an Afro. He had been assigned to teach history and English at a high school which taught both girls and boys at the higher levels. The lower grades taught only boys. His eye fell on a chemistry teacher called Salma. That the name resonated with recent events back home did not escape him, it intrigued him further. "I thought it was fate," he explains drily, his hand adjusting the ghost of a tobacco pipe at his mouth. "But she was pretty—wow! And she still is." My mother smiles an acknowledgement, and he looks away, pleased with himself. It took time and much effort to woo Salma, Miss Tamim. She would not go out with him, always coming up with a cheerful refusal and some bland excuse. One day, finally, she declared to him what should have been obvious: "My family would not like me going out at night, and especially with a man." "Because I'm not a Muslim?" he asked. "Any man," she replied. Especially a foreigner, but she did not tell him that. Her grandfather was a well-known sheikh, forever preaching morals to his flock. But it was evident that she liked him. All the girls and even the boys liked him: he was American, with an easy confidence and a way of speaking they found funny but charming, having heard it only in the movies. Frank Sinatra, Elvis, John Wayne, Sidney Poitier. The girls nicknamed him Sidney Poitier, though with his round face he looked nothing like the actor. He took the compliment.

His chance came not long after that exchange. *The Crucible* was playing at the appropriately named Little Theatre, the only one in town, and the schools received invitations to send their English classes to see it. Martin would need a female teacher to go with his girls, and he applied to the headmaster for help. He suggested Miss Tamim's name as the possible escort. Salma had no choice. At the theatre he lavished her with attention. After the play he drove her home in the little car he had bought, but first they stopped over at the Palm Beach Hotel for soft drinks and halal snacks. They discussed the play. They discussed America. Civil rights. Malcolm X had travelled in Africa, though he missed Tanzania, and Stokely Carmichael had only recently visited. Chinua Achebe was expected very soon.

"I was smitten," she says wistfully. "I had liked him anyway, but now I was truly in love. I had never met a person, man or woman, so considerate. So passionate about the world, and about Black-ness . . . Of course, he was courting me then, but still."

These two have maintained that electricity between them. The wattage may be low, but it keeps on glowing. My eyes hold hers. She's greyed and seems smaller now but has retained her long face and lean features. We never mention the Arab blood in her ancestry. We always celebrate Christmas, and in Philadelphia she attends church with my grandmother, but she says her Muslim prayer as soon as she wakes up every day and keeps a Quran by her bedside. Dad used to join her in her prayer sometimes, but he's given up. I used to join her too when I was little.

"Where do I come in?" I ask and break the silence.

"Coming to that," says Dad. "We thought you should know the full story."

There followed clandestine meetings, after school and early in the morning at a tea shack behind the school. They wanted to get married. You should talk to my folks, she said. So one bright Sunday morning at around eleven Martin went to see Sheikh Bushiri Tamim to ask for his granddaughter's hand. The sheikh had already been told by Salma's mother that the Black American was to come. He sat on an old sofa before a coffee table having his kahawa; he told Dad to sit down opposite and offered him a cup. And then my dad spoke, in broken Swahili; the old man knew some English, and Salma's father was the standby. The sheikh wanted to know everything about Dad, his family, his ancestry, his religion and politics. He asked him why he wanted to marry someone outside his culture. Dad told him he loved Salma, and he believed there was a strong bond in their both being African. The old man smiled; neither Mom nor Dad can say what could have been in his mind, but he told Dad to return the following Friday, after the midday prayer.

"I was annoyed, but she told me I must have made a good impression. He could have dismissed me straightaway as a nonbeliever and fake African."

On Friday my dad went to Salma's house, this time taking a gift of a Quran with him. Both my dad and the sheikh had done their research; the sheikh had sent his spies to find out everything they could about this American teacher; and Martin had inquired about Qurans and bought a calligraphed copy he could hardly afford from an Indian trader. Sheikh Tamim asked Dad if he was willing to become a Muslim. Dad had discussed this with Salma; he was an agnostic, but figured that if Malcolm could become Malik Shabazz, and Cassius Clay was now Muhammad Ali, why couldn't Martin Stewart adopt a Muslim name for love's sake? He became Baraka Stewart. And they had a proper Swahili wedding, with jasmine flowers and ululations and a trumpet procession through Salma's neighbourhood.

Now comes my story proper. Dad pauses, and Mom stirs in her seat and looks away, then turns to me with affection. She stretches her hand out towards me, I take it.

She became pregnant, but delivered a stillborn at the local hospital. As they sat in her ward, grief-stricken at the news, a junior nurse approached them.

"She told us there was a young Indian mother with a child she could not afford to keep," Dad says, slowly.

"Why?"

"She was single and poor. There were social considerations."

"So you took me to replace your dead baby? It was that easy?"

"The doctor was not there—too busy or simply looked away—and the nurse simply brought in the child in a bassinet. A beautiful baby."

"And the other baby?"

That catches him short. "A boy." Their child. But what could they have done, he was dead. If he had lived, he would be the one with a grandmother in Philadelphia, and all those relations, he would not be conflicted like I am now.

Immediately after Salma was discharged, they started having qualms. They found out about the girl's parents and went to visit them, taking with them the child. Me. The girl's father was a local shoemaker. Mom reads out his name from a small piece of paper and hands it to me: *Jairam Solanki and Shanti Behn.* My real grandparents. My hand starts to shake uncontrollably, and I seize it with the other and clamp it down. I am crying for a reason I cannot understand, and they watch me helplessly.

"Mr. and Mrs. Solanki were grateful to us," Dad says. "We were a godsend. The girl would have been ostracized, the child too, and he would have had no future."

I look at the paper in my hand. Under the couple's name is another one, in crooked writing. "And this one under it—is that a name?"

They both nod.

"My mother?"

Dad says, "Yes. Your biological mother."

Sushila.

"It's a Hindi name?"

"Indian. Hindu, yes."

I was born an Indian, they brought me up as African American. I was born a Hindu, I am now a nonpracticing Muslim. What name would she have had in mind? Is this why my shoes never quite fit, are too narrow or too big?—reminding me that I don't quite belong? I look at this willowy woman with greying hair, preferring long dresses in retirement and the colours orange, black, and green; and this man who calls himself Baraka because he loves her, preferring his old grey cardigan unbuttoned, and his ghost pipe at his mouth, my mom and dad. They have stepped back a little. And I feel strangely alone.

I book an Acela to New York for the afternoon.

Sushila

I was the precocious one. Hormones, they call it now. Wanting to be loved by a man, like in the movies. Romance. The manager at Odeon Cinema would let Ma and me sneak in sometimes, because Bapu was the one who made his shoes. They fitted him just right, he said. All his customers said that; they called him Fit-right Mochi.

First there was that Ashok, whom I would meet on the roof of their building down the road after school in the afternoon. The adults would be relaxing having tea in their shops downstairs and the coast was clear. It was a quiet hour. We would play all sorts of romantic games. I will be Dilip, you Madhubala. Like this. Let me touch you here. They will grow soon. And then, They do it like this in English films. Lip-touch. Tongue-touch. He was a sly one, but I let him. And what a whipping he got, and the whipping I got, when a servant saw us and reported. He was sent to India to get himself cleansed. Bathe in the Ganges and so on.

What brought this on? This memory of Ashok? Oh yes, a letter from an American girl who's just returned from Tanzania. Jogging another memory, one I could do without.

It happened a year or two after Ashok and was the silliest thing a girl could do. The riskiest thing. Suicidal. One Sunday in December, the sun beating down without mercy, I was returning home from Urmila Auntie in Upanga, carrying a basketful of shoes to be repaired by my father. It was a lonely patch of road, and a boy went racing past me on a bicycle, coming quite close. He suddenly braked up ahead, and I remember his bicycle wobbled as he did so. He turned around and came back towards me. A handsome boy, hair like Elvis, fair-skinned. He had come to our shop to have his feet measured for shoes. "Cobbler's daughter, no? Do you want a ride? Lovely girl like you, baking in this sun? Do you want to look dark like an African? Hop on." I did just that, knowing I shouldn't. I sat at the back, but crafty fellow, after a short distance he says with a grin, "The carrier isn't good, the wires will only poke your bottom. Come sit on the bar here in the front." And this silly girl obeys. He took a long route, rubbing me shamelessly from behind, squeezing me tight with his upper arms, I can still picture it, and we stopped at a large shady tree. Behind it, facing away from the path.

And then mysteriously, the following months, no periods. Ma, what's wrong? Bapu comes inside and interrogates me, demanding the name of the bastard who did this, and he beats me with a shoe. They give me a pair of kitchen tongs to insert and remove the fetus, as if it was a piece of charcoal. But I am three months and showing a little. Ma sees the panic on my face, and says, "No. Stop. Don't make her put anything inside her that will poison her. We'll keep her in hiding." For six months I was a prisoner in the back room, along with old discarded shoes and clothes and scraps of leather, cans of glue, and rats and cockroaches. How it smelled. There was an old shoemaker's last that I played with and spoke to and used to beat down the cockroaches. I could come out for washing only at night and dawn. I remember reading scraps of old newspapers. Mantras were said on me. Ma would light incense and recite aartis. A priest came late one night and spent hours reciting over me, even when I had fallen asleep. Bapu lost weight. And I wanted to kill myself. Just let me walk down to the seashore, Bapu, it's only half a mile away, and I will drown myself. All our troubles will be over. He looked at me. Seemed to contemplate. "Perhaps when you were born," he muttered, "we should have done that. A big mistake."

And then the time came. Flutters in the belly. What shall I do, Ma? Bapu went and pleaded with Dr. Malek, swore her to secrecy. "Where can we take her, Doctor?" "Don't worry, Jairam Bhai," she told him. "These things happen. You made such good shoes for me to take away to college in Poona. You brought them to my home just as I was leaving for the airport." She had a room prepared for me at the European Hospital, facing the sea. And she delivered the baby herself, and this baby came out almost painless, and she held it up and handed it to my mother, and I never saw it again. A nice couple wanted a child, they were desperate. "Boy or girl, Ma?" "It's better not to know more. Think that nothing happened. It was all a dream and it has gone away."

And so it did. Whenever the thought came, of that baby, an image of that little curled-up body and that scrunched-up little face, I would push it away. For the shame of it. For my stupidity. For that little bit of anxiety pushing itself out: Is he all right? Alive? Now I know he was a she, and she is all right.

Was it all that stupid? For the time, yes it was. Nowadays they go about freely, the youngsters, expressing themselves. There are precautions. There is advice.

After that . . . time . . . with the boy with the Elvis hair, the sweaty smell . . . he was handsome, strong, and murmured all kinds of endearments as he took me . . . I imagined, hoped and dreamed he would come for me, send a marriage proposal. But he didn't even pick up his shoes, Bapu sent them with our servant, who returned with the money. Bapu could have guessed, but he was a bit of a coward. Cobblers had no status. But the boy never showed up. And strangely, I never saw him again . . . Did I enjoy it? It was a sensation, yes, though it hurt. "Your husband will not do it with such love," he had panted into my ear. And then, as he dropped me off, "Use Vicks if it hurts." He had called me *darling* in English! The cheek.

What do I tell this American girl, who claims she is my daughter and wants to come and meet me? It's not worth the trouble. Her real mother and father are the ones who brought her up to be as clever as she seems to be. What would I do with this new complication? Her name is Zakia.

SPEAK SWEET WORDS, SOFTLY

1. DAR ES SALAAM.

The girl.

Meet my loving gaze, Raheem, show me that compassion that is your name. I've fallen in love, young man, with your mischievous gait and alluring face. Oh darling, dearest, my body quivers with desire, have mercy on me. I will walk a thousand miles for you, I will write a hundred love letters to you, all the time I sing this song to you.

He is eighteen years old, they say, the young lord arrived from abroad, newly anointed, his face beaming grace, his voice smooth and foreign, his enunciations clear, his advice to young and old intelligent and compassionate. He is the one I want to love, he is the one I want for my husband. But he is

God, how can you say that, that's blasphemy! You'll burn in hell. But I'm already burning, can't you see, I'm in hell until he comes and picks me up and rescues me.

I see him walking on air over the ground in his white suit and white shoes, his gait light as a feather, the angels shower him with glitter, women in white throw red and pink petals upon him . . . he is the holiest of the holy and he sees down through the seven earths and up into the seven heavens and he can see my sin, but I see him step down and I desire him, I cannot sleep and desire him, I sweat and wet myself and desire him, I am in his arms and he caresses me and . . . what can I do? For God's sake, for his sake, what can I do?

The parents.

"We will send a plea to him, he is all-knowing and in his mercy surely he will cure our daughter."

"We will send offerings to the prayer house, and every Sunday we will feed fourteen girls and wash their feet and give them each a gift of a handkerchief and a coin, we will be generous to the beggars. We will feed the kids at the orphanage. Every day at noon, standing on one foot I will pray to him. Lord, only preserve my daughter. Save her. Keep her pure and sinless."

"And if she is cured I will pick a Friday and give one shilling to everyone who sets foot in our shop that day."

"But why this test upon us, what have we done to deserve this curse? After years of want and struggle, when finally we were beginning to do well, now this calamity."

"He knows best, we cannot know his ways. It's a test. We can simply pray."

The maalim.

The maalim's house is a mud affair, I grew up in just such a house. There are people waiting as we arrive, sitting on the ground quietly in the front room, all looking desperate. Most of them women. Why does God affect us women so? We are weak in the emotions . . . if only I had borne a son instead of this daughter. The maalim sits in one corner, chanting behind a cloud of incense from a brazier. Why does he keep smiling? Doesn't anything trouble him? Does everything amuse him? The dry, cracked floor feels cool on our bare feet, the wall is rough and scratches the back when we sit down. "Come forward," says the maalim to her, smelling money, "get up and come forward here," and she gets up and takes the place just vacated before him and meets his eyes across the smoking brazier.

"What ails you? You do not look well. Do you speak non-sense at home? Tell me, daughter."

"I love him, he's my lover," she speaks words I've never heard from her before, and the maalim says, "Whom do you love, my daughter?"

"I love God."

"The imam! That is good!—like a husband?—that is bad! You go to pray to the temple?"

"Yes. To our mosque."

"Now, my daughter, I understand, he's a handsome man, your lord, and he's rich, but he's beyond you, far far away from you where he has beautiful white angels attending him, and I must cure you and bring you to the straight and narrow called *siratal*. Do you understand?"

"Yes."

"Now what has caused you all this trouble? You must have walked under a mbuyu tree. You must have been out at the hour of *magharab*, when it is neither night nor day and the spirits slip down into the world. And one of them entered this pretty girl and turned himself into a lascivious woman. A woman with desires. Desires that are not appropriate. Yes?"

"Yes."

"I will pray for you."

He brings out a small book the size of his palm, its pages loose and yellow with age, and starts reciting from it, rocking his head back and forth and he goes on and goes on and I think he's forgotten himself and my ankle bones are hurting and my daughter looks dreamy but suddenly he winds down to a stop. He gives her some water to drink from a tray. He gives her roots to chew and collects the chewed remnants and puts them aside. He gives her roots to take home to boil in water and drink the tea. He walks her to the door and I follow behind. Outside where it's brilliant with sun he asks me for his gift. I place in his hand a fat wad of bills that I've brought with me.

The girl.

Walking, walking I am tired now, I cannot bear this ache any longer. Over rock and thorn, through fire and smoke. My lord, come and save me. Place your hand on my head, embrace me, Raheem, cast your loving gaze upon me and recognize my devotion. Make me your slave, I will sweep the floor under your feet with my hair, I will clean after you, I will lick your plate when you've eaten. I cannot bear it any longer. Stay in my breast, my lord. Stay in my soul, my husband. There is no one else.

The parents.

"We've tried everything. We can only wait for our prayers to be answered."

"But I wonder . . . I fear . . ."

"Yes, dear?"

"Is it right . . ."

"What?"

"After beseeching our lord so much for his help, to try other means too? Visiting the maalim. And others. It shows we don't have faith."

"We have faith. He knows. He understands our weakness. Perhaps indirectly it's he who told us to go to these people. But in the end, it's all in his hands."

"Or the Devil's. We've come under his shadow."

"But God always wins. Keep faith."

The girl.

I beseech you, my lord, turn to me with a smile. I humble myself before you, master of my soul, king of my heart, my raja. Show me a glimpse of you, Karsan!

The potter woman.

The potters' colony is a ramshackle compound inside a gate. We enter and we could be in India. Poor and backward.

"Come, dear," I tell her, "we'll follow this man. And don't look about at the others. They have shifty eyes. Look how modestly the women are covered, going about their work. And you are in a short dress. They are not used to that. Come. But this squelchy mud is like clay, sticks to the chappals—be careful, don't slip—hold my hand. They must dump their unused clay right here, where people walk, couldn't find a better place."

"Come," the man says as we reach a shack, "go inside, my mother is there, she will heal you. She has the power."

Inside, an old woman sits on the floor before a fire baking rotla, shaping the millet dough with her hands, each piece a perfect disk as it should be, and throws it on the earthen taawli. My girl looks on in wonder. "Isn't this how I've taught you to make them?" I murmur. "I know," she says.

The ma's wrinkled face glows red, and she's so tiny.

"Come, my daughters, come inside," she bids us and wobbles off towards an inner room.

"What about the rotla, ma?" I ask.

"Don't worry, my daughter-in-law will come to attend them."

And I thought I was short, look at her, barely up to my shoulders. And they don't even have a bed, they sleep on the floor. No chairs, one stool before the mirror. Straw mat on the floor.

"Tell me, dear," says the ma, peering into her face. "So what ails you? So pale!" She runs her fingers lightly over my daughter's face.

"She eats well. Even meat!" I protest.

"Even so, there's a paleness in her. Her soul aches. What ails you, dear?"

"I love him . . ."

"She's in love. Forbidden love?"

"Yes."

"Father?"

"No!—she's in love with our imam, I don't know which is worse!"

"Imam? Tch, tch. Not good. Come with me to the back. Not you, mother. You will cast a shadow on her. Stay here."

Soon they return.

"What have you done to my girl, she's all wet."

"I've cleansed her and given her some herbs to take. Her *there* is raw, down below. Her nipples are raw. I've given her medicines."

The mother.

"What did she do?"

"She prayed over me, in a strange language. Like a crazy song."

"And? How did you get wet?"

"She cleaned me."

"Where? . . . Even *there*? Why did she say it was raw?"

"I don't know."

"What have you done to yourself?"

"Nothing."

"You be careful, or you won't ever bear children! She gave you medicine for that? I'll throw it away. We'll buy calamine lotion. The old Hindu charlatan. Low-caste mischief-maker. Making fools of us. Perverse."

The girl.

The fort is high and strong, it rises to the sky, and I'm a forlorn fish in the moat below. Lord, descend and fetch me, I'm losing my mind with love. My darling, come to me, my husband, come to me, forgive me if I lapsed for a moment . . . My family are my prison. Who can know the truth of my body's agony, my heart's anguish? My darling, come to me, my husband, come to me. Forgive if I've offended.

The parents.

"No, it did not work. All the way there for nothing. Who was it that recommended her? Why do you listen to people and send me all over?"

"What do we do, then? That old woman has cured people of jaundice and the evil eye. My brother's daughter; both the neighbour's children, they almost died of blackwater fever. She has a reputation in town."

"What reputation. Magic won't work, I have told you. You want to send her to all sorts of people, Hindus and Muslims and whoever, and what will they turn my girl into? Oh, Lord, what sins have I committed . . ."

"Don't cry now, they're just trying to help . . . Listen, they say there's an American. Don't look so. A doctor of the mind."

"Of the mind?"

"Yes. Of the mind. The *Standard* says he's the only one in the whole country."

"How can that be? You need a degree, don't you, to get into the mind?"

"He has degrees. The *Standard* says the whole of Class 12 in a Kampala school fainted last month during assembly. All at the same time. All girls. And this white man was sent there and cured them."

The American psychiatrist.

"Hi . . . Hello."

"Hello."

"I'm Dr. Preston."

"Dr. Preston."

"Yes, and I'm here to help you. Do you understand? . . . Good. Sit down here, where I can see you. Now tell me, what is it that's bothering you?"

"I'm in love with him . . ."

"With . . . your spiritual leader? . . ."

He looks at her parents, they've told him.

"You nod, so you agree. That is nothing to worry about. It happens to young people, falling in love with adults. Hey, why are you crying? What makes you so unhappy?"

"I want him to love me back . . ."

"How? Can you tell me how you want him to love you? . . . You see him in your dreams?"

She nods up and down.

"Okay. Do you imagine him? What do you see then?"

"Kissing his feet . . . and he lifts me up and looks me in the eyes . . . and he . . ."

"Takes you in his arms? Not everyone can love us back. We sometimes love impossible people when we are young. Actors. Do you know how many girls your age love Elvis? Scream for him? Pull out their hair—you don't do that, do you? Paul McCartney? There, you see. You are just like many girls. Just don't take it too seriously, think of other things. Do you like to read novels?"

"No."

"Listen to music?"

"Yes."

"Well, when you get these feelings, listen to music. Sing. You have a brother and sister, yes?—play with them. Tell jokes to each other. Parents make a good subject—they can be funny, yes? And then come and see me in two weeks—understand? Two weeks—and tell me how it went. You can tell me anything you want. Anything you say will be in confidence—no one else will know. Not even your mother and father. Understand?"

The girl.

When the swami comes the drum will resound,
lights will glitter in all the directions
to welcome him.
How do we fall at his feet?
His lover broke her chain of pearls
and went down on her knees to pick them up.

"Thank him, he's back. Now listen, daughter. Don't look him in the eye. Never look the lord in the eye. His power can affect you. Just bow your head before him, keep saying the prayer in your mind, and let him put his hand on your back and bless you. Say Amen. And then walk on but not showing your back to him. Can you do it? And then your problem will go away. Forget all those charlatans."

But I met his eyes and he understood. I met his eyes and he smiled. His look said *I love you* in return. *It's just that I am busy and tied up and they don't leave me alone. I am needed by everyone. They all love me.* I met his eyes.

—

2. MANHATTAN, NEW YORK.

The girl.

"Hey, baby, want to have a good time?"

She hurries on.

"Hey, where you from? India? *Hare Rama*? You want to see America? I can show you. All right, you don't want to go away. Like the Big Apple, hey? . . . Listen, baby. You want to make quick cash? Moolah, mucho moolah. You understand?"

"You're hurting me!"

"Hey, leave her alone. Here, can I take you home? I won't hurt you. Where do you live? . . . Twenty-Sixth. And? Lexington. All right—here—get into this cab. Driver, Twenty-Sixth and Lex. Bye, Miss. You should be careful of strangers. This is New York."

George.

She sees him a few days later on Third Avenue.

"Hi, Miss—remember me? On Seventh?—Outside Macy's? I put you in a cab."

It takes her a moment to recall. "Yes . . ."

"My name is George, I live on Twenty-Eighth Street. I guess we are neighbours! I was going for coffee—would you like to have coffee?"

"Yes," she says, and it just so happens that she runs into him every so often. They become friends. Her first friend in America. And they talk.

"I'm looking for a job, you know."

"Yes, New York's expensive. What brought you to New York? Student?"

"No, tourist."

"You must be very adventurous!"

"I just walked into here," she says.

"What do you mean, you walked into here? To New York!"

"I came at the airport, they stopped me, told me to wait. They took my passport."

"You had a visa?"

"Yes, but still. The man was rude. He didn't believe me that I was a tourist."

"And?"

"He went away to talk to someone, and I just walked out. I left and nobody stopped me."

"You entered illegally."

"Yes. I think so. Is that bad?"

"No, I don't think so."

"And now I have no passport."

He helped her get a job at a cousin's bath and kitchen shop on Forty-Eighth. He took her to an immigration lawyer way up on 113th. She made a few friends at work. She became a New Yorker.

"I like you a lot," says George one day, in her apartment. He's carried her groceries. "I guess you know that. You are very attractive. And gentle, not like these American girls, all pushy."

"I like you too, George."

"I think we make a good couple," he says. "I guess we've never been quite . . . intimate. Can we try?"

He leans forward and as she cringes inside he kisses her delicately on a cheek and she blushes deeply. Her heart beats so fast she thinks she's having a heart attack. A man touching her. But it didn't feel bad. It takes a few days before he tries to land a kiss on her lips. She pulls away.

"I can't, George."

He withdraws.

"I'm sorry. I didn't mean to upset you." She smiles her thanks.

"I guess you don't like me that way . . ."

"I like you, George, but."

"There's someone you've left behind? Someone there?"

She doesn't reply at first, then whispers yes.

"That's fine, then we'll still be friends. Okay?"

"Thanks George."

The girl.

There's no one anywhere but you, my lord. I depend on you to preserve me, just as you came to Draupadi's aid when she called your name . . .

But he's no devil, George is a saint, just so you know, and he keeps me company, without making demands, no need to get jealous! I have no one else here, nobody to talk to, except George. There have been attacks on women recently, and he calls to check on me. He even comes with me to the Indian restaurant on Lexington, sometimes, but poor fellow, he can't tolerate the spices and eats only rice and yogurt. Even there, the men gawk at me. George noticed, warned me to be careful not to be followed. One day we went to the top of the Empire State Building, and it was wonderful!—but you couldn't see too far because of the smog. It's not the tallest building anymore, he told me, there are two new ones on the other side of the city, and we could just see them, as shadowy, ghostly figures.

The girl and her sister.

"Thank God you are here. I don't know what I would have done. It gets so lonely sometimes. Sundays, especially." How many Sundays has she cried herself to sleep, but she doesn't tell her sister that. "But I've become quite the New Yorker. Here you walk fast, did you notice that? It's automatic, you just do it! . . . Did they stop you at Immigration?"

"No, I said I had come to see my sister, and they let me in."

"You have your passport, then."

"Yes, I have my passport. How come you lost yours?"

"Long story. Real adventure."

"What's the apartment like?"

"All right. But cockroaches, you have to help me get rid of them."

"Cockroaches? In New York? Are you serious?"

"Yes. Now first thing, you have to find a job. Then we go to this lawyer who can help us . . .Tell me, how are Ma and Bapa?"

"They are well. And happy you are settling and have a job. You sound like a real American in your letters! Every day they give thanks to God. And I do too. But who's this George? We are all curious! I thought our parents would have a fit when you wrote about him, but they didn't mind. They want you to be happy. They always favoured you."

"Don't be silly. Yes, he was a nice guy I met accidentally. He was very nice to me, he found me the job and the lawyer who's doing our green cards . . ."

"And?"

"He had to go to Puerto Rico to take over his father's business . . . they have a factory there . . ."

"And?—you let him go?"

They walk in silence.

"I made a mistake, I know."

Her sister says nothing.

"I just couldn't . . . I liked him but I couldn't. I would like to go to California. The weather is better and there's the sea. I heard it's nice. Not so dirty like New York."

The scholar.

"In our sacred songs," I explained to her, "the singer takes on the persona of a woman, a lover, even when he's a man. But he's a lover of God. That is a well-known trope in mystical literature. The devotee as the female lover."

"And women?" she asked, a little aggressively.

"Women too, though somehow that seems normal. Some of the songs are intensely longing and very sensuous."

She stared at me. Of course she knew all that, I was just carried away and showing off. I smiled at her.

"My sister liked to sing them. She had a lovely voice."

"Really? I'm sure you sing well too."

"But she was exceptional. She sang whenever she could."

Her tone had fallen, and I didn't know what to say.

"But she took it literally—this lover bit. She thought she was a real lover of our lord—who is very handsome, as you know. She could not separate her reality from this trope, as you call it. She became depressed. It was hard to see her like that. She couldn't control herself."

Her voice drifted and she looked away. In an afterthought, she picked up her handbag and brought out from it a snapshot to show to me. The girl in the picture was fair and not very tall, with long hair and a plain face that was strikingly beautiful.

"Where is she now?" I asked softly.

She didn't answer for some moments, then: "She went to Santa Monica in California. Stayed there for two years."

"And where did she go from there?"

"She found her lord at last . . . she drowned herself at high tide."

"Don't cry, please . . . she's found her peace."

But that story has haunted me since. I can't forget it, and that face, I can't quite explain why. I thought that one day I'd write about it.

The girl.

Speak sweet words, softly . . . the lord is the Ganges in which you drown. In her heart he resides forever, and she cannot sleep or stay awake . . .

My lord, one day I became afraid. I was older and not so good-looking. I had to extract a tooth. And you remained radiant and handsome as ever. How your face shone in your new photos. But more and more you ignored me. Once, you had looked into my eyes and showed you understood my agony of love. You were helpless, you said. But now you're married to a most beautiful European model, what could I be to you? I will no longer haunt your dreams nor you mine.

THE KING OF COTTON

My grandfather adores me. "Why do you love me so much, Dada?" I inquire, braking to a stop before him, putting my hands on his knees. His twinkling face breaks into a barely audible laugh that squeaks out like a loose spring inside his throat. He tickles my chin. "Wait till you make children of your own," he says. "There's nothing like it."

He looks around for confirmation, sees my dadi, who exchanges a look with him but says not a word.

"I don't want children or grandchildren, Dada!"

"You will."

What I would have liked is a father.

As I back off and run away our eyes avoid each other's that instant, except for a tiny flash from one corner of my eye to a corner in his. There's an understanding. An accusation and a terrible admission.

He sits back, his eyes following me.

That large oval head, those few white wisps of hair like a feathery, tentative halo on its gleaming top. His beautiful face, that's how it's always been for me, ageing minutely, always smooth, just a little older with the years. Unlike Dadi, with her ashen face and head like an old cardboard box weathered and dented by the years, a far cry from the blushing bride of their wedding photo.

The doting Dada of my childhood I've come to think of as my father's murderer. I don't believe in the supernatural, and perhaps it's his own guilt that informed my indictment the years I knew him. He had never forgiven himself, I know, nor did anyone else, this man the fruits of whose once-ruthless enterprise in Africa we now live on in Canada like maggots on dead flesh, who sat flicking the remote control morning till night, willing death to come from some channel, only it wouldn't. But when it came finally, it was to everyone's relief.

The family, like many others, had come penniless from India to East Africa in the early 1900s. Through their business acumen, imprinted on their Gujarati genes, so we believe, they managed to lift themselves up in the alien country and make it home. Three meals a day and no debtors knocking at the door with their collection books; comfortable, no more than that, but only a few such pioneers could boast that luxury. Dada inherited the family business, distributing potatoes, onions, and various grains. Not glamorous, and I understand that the shop stank up the street in the rainy season so that people sometimes were forced to take an alternative route. But a steady enterprise, nonetheless. It could have gone on for decades more. But one day fortune came his way, as it did the Canadian who looked under his tire when he was stuck on a muddy road somewhere in the interior of the country and saw a diamond. Thus began the Williamson Diamond Mines. This part of our story we proudly discuss, embellish, and throw around. How do you know when opportunity is looking you in the face? You know, if you're my dada. He knew how to look, as did Mr. Williamson.

Dada was obsessed with news, anything that was happening, anywhere in the world. War and peace, famine and abundance, royal weddings and births. The daily paper reached him at five every morning. Later, on his midmorning break from office, before chai and bhajias at the K T shop, he would saunter in at the Indian reading room and peruse newspapers from around the world. Even if they were weeks late. Knowledge gained, instinct sharpened. At the chai shop later, discussion and argument on all the news that had been fit to see print, plus the previous night's BBC broadcast. All talk about elsewhere, nothing much happened in that backwater. The War in Europe had no impact, except for a few shortages of imported items. Some speculation in property went on; a little gambling and drinking, though forbidden; fornication. When the War ended, the price of sisal, which was used to make sacking and rope, suddenly dropped. The Germans and Greeks who had owned the sisal farms, the Germans having brought the crop to the country in the first place during their rule, started leaving, tired, elderly, and bankrupt. Defeated. Dada, my family says, had already seen in the newspapers the portents of another war, and so he and his friends bought up the abandoned sisal properties at dirt-cheap prices. And sure enough, the Korean War began, and sisal shot up again. Fortunes were made.

They lived like kings thenceforth. Bungalows by the sea, servants, exotic foods, when the rest of their Indian community still lived in shacks with holes for toilets. They travelled abroad, acquired a polished veneer, their children went to study abroad and came home speaking English like the English. A new social class formed. Sisal eventually fell when nylon came around, but by then they were ready to walk away from it. Dada was into cotton, Suleman Rawji and Sons importing it from America and India with a monopoly. You want raw cotton—Marikani—from America, you go to Suleman Rawji. You want to stock the khanga wraparound, weaved and printed in India with the latest brilliant African designs and catchy Swahili proverbs, Suleman is your man. The monument to his success was the art deco building at the bustling corner of Market and Mosque streets, five floors high with a dozen shops and fifty apartments. Suleman Rawji Building, the biggest one in town, only to be nationalized in less than two decades by a socialist government.

He sits, this former king in economic exile, in a house in North Vancouver, on his La-Z-Boy in his pyjamas all day, the Indian way. Hoping, I suppose, that one of his grandchildren will visit today. He arrives at a news channel, watches a few minutes, pauses at a soccer match, then quickly heads on, past CNN, Fox, and local Punjabi, and rests a moment longer at NDTV from Delhi. Nothing holds him. He takes a nap, gently snores. He used to drive, but now can't, due to recurring gout. He takes a taxi sometimes to go to a community function or the Safari chai shop, which is the news and nostalgia exchange, where former cricket players from Dar come to recall their best innings, and visitors from Toronto are welcomed and mocked: do you have such chai, such kababs and bhajias in your city? Most of the time he sits at home flipping channels. His time is past, his money given away to his two sons, two daughters, and one widowed daughter-in-law, my mother.

One late afternoon—I must assume it was Sunday, though Dadi will not confirm—there was a garden party on the grounds of their Oyster Bay mansion in Dar es Salaam, at which several VIPs, including the British governor of the territory, Sir Edward Twining, and the colonial secretary, Iain Macleod, on a tour from London, were present. Between these two eminences stood the cotton king displaying his charm, while a pleasant, sophisticated murmur proceeded in the background. Suddenly a commotion was heard at the gate. Sporadic recriminations and exclamations of protest approached the party, and the guests saw an old woman in rags in the tight clutches of two watchmen, who were dragging her forward. When she was close enough, she broke loose and hurled herself through the guests and ran up straight to Suleman Rawji. A hush fell, as the woman raised her hands before the king of cotton in a gesture of prayer. Please.

"My son is dead and waiting to be buried, I cannot find a cotton sheet to wrap him in. Help me! *Msada, mfalme wangu! Tafadhali, Sulemani.* Two yards of Marikani is all I need!"

In his arrogance, bloated by the presence of two white men of the British government at his side, Suleman Rawji asked her angrily to repeat her request, then told her with contempt, "Mama, if you don't have money to buy two yards of cotton, use grass to shroud your son! How dare you disturb me here in my home? Go away."

Her arms dropped to her sides. Her little eyes were moist. The chocolate skin on her face was so wrinkled it fell in folds. Her bare feet were covered in dust. Humiliated by fate and now this Indian. At another time he might have relented, he was known to soften. But this time he had to show his pride, demonstrate to all those present what stern stuff the cotton king Suleman Rawji was made of. Wealth didn't come to you just like that.

The watchmen pulled the supplicant away, but not before she turned and exclaimed:

"Suleman, I curse you! I curse you. Today you deny me two yards of Marikani to bury my son. You, Suleman, I tell you, you will not even see your son's burial!"

The sons were all there, three of them, standing among the fashionable crowd. Their pretty wives were there too, and some smartly clad children, running about.

This was the story told to me by Dadi, long after they had moved to Vancouver. She told it sounding matter-of-fact. But in that toneless voice, in that lowering gaze hid the regret, the blame. Like arsenic dissolved in plain water. Curses had power, Suleman knew that. And yet, adamantly, he refused to go and have the spell reversed. "We make our own luck," he said. "And I pay my dues to God. Who else has the power to change my luck? An old beggar? If she had power, why was she in rags, a stinking destitute?"

Belgian Congo next door, across Lake Tanganyika, was one of the first African countries to become independent. Patrice Lumumba was the first prime minister, I studied that in a college course. Following his death, or assassination as many believe, war raged in that country that doesn't seem to have stopped to this day. For the businessmen, this was opportunity: supplies were scarce—soap, sugar, flour, and oil; canned food and spices. Profits were high, and the armies had money. You remained safe because you brought in the essentials and paid off all sides for protection. In any case, you had some young clerk, fresh off the boat from India or from a poor family upcountry, to be your front man. You were the king, safe in your castle far away by the sea.

It was my father Pyarali's turn to make the monthly visit to Bukavu, eastern Congo, to check on the family businesses there. Pyarali was the youngest of three brothers and two sisters. The journey was by chartered plane, its passengers a few businessmen and accountants. As usual for such visits, they took with them fresh supplies to stock the shops, and—a rumour never denied to this day—they would bring back pouches filled with smuggled diamonds together with their bags of cash from the previous month's sales. It was Pyarali's second such trip, but this time the plane disappeared on its way in. The pilot being a young American, the search that ensued was thorough and followed by the public. Two airplanes and a helicopter were chartered for the purpose. Men and women were paid to beat the bushes around their villages. (Outside one village a few people were attacked by a leopard.) The pilot's parents and a sister from America and Suleman Rawji with his men covered the countryside in Land Rovers, in northern Tanganyika and western Uganda where the plane was believed to have disappeared. Prayers were said in the temples of worship in various towns and cities. A few months after the disappearance, when the search had been called off, a fragment of a small plane's wing was found in a field in Uganda, having become a play object for children.

A service without a corpse was finally held in the compound of the khano, our prayer house. There, as Dada stood before the empty coffin, which was draped with a white cotton sheet, his remaining sons and two brothers beside him, their hands raised for the recital of the fateha, and a large congregation behind them, the women wailing and not only those from the family, a voice approached from behind.

"Weh Sulemani! Do you remember! Ten years ago I asked you for a shroud . . ." The old lady shuffled forward, more wrinkled and bent than before, hardly a curly hair left on the head. A finger raised. ". . . You refused. *Ulikataa!* And I cursed you. Your son will not even have a burial . . . I told you."

She came forward and Suleman Rawji made room for her in the front row.

Dadi said a chill ran down her spine as the woman spoke. She let out a scream and wailed uncontrollably. And I suppose she's still crying inside.

Remember, we don't talk about it. Nothing happened except Pyarali died in a plane crash tragically when his wife was pregnant with the youngest. It was only this one time, when Dadi and I were alone, that she told me the story, just for the record, and to teach me a lesson. Even kings fall.

THE WAY STOP

Joseph and I got off our bus at Nasingwe, nursing a lingering disappointment at a journey aborted, or rather, reversed. Three days before, like a pair of excited schoolboys we had left Dar es Salaam and headed down south along the Tanzanian coast for Lindi, a once thriving historic town halfway to the Mozambique border. The Germans had their regional centre here a century ago, in colonial times; I recalled it having a competitive school cricket team. Now it bore all the signs of hard times and neglect. The economic boom had happened further south. Spending a night here, we took another transport, more local than the first, and headed inland west for the junction town of Masasi, with the intention of connecting to Songea, then going onward north to Iringa and Dodoma in the heart of the country, and finally east back to Dar. There was not a little satisfaction to be had in completing the loop, to say we had gone to the south of the country and around. But even before the Masasi junction, the portents had begun to look bleak, when we had to walk barefoot on a section of the road running through a seasonal lake where we were told—rightly or wrongly—a female crocodile had come to seek rest the previous year. At Masasi our fears were confirmed when we learned that the road onward to Songea, running through dense forest, was damaged from the rain; only open four-wheel drives ventured out, which meant the certain prospect of breakdowns and mosquitoes and the not unlikely possibility of meeting lions or leopards. Reluctantly, we had turned around on the only bus available that day. It was bound, hugging the border along the Ruvuma River, for the coastal boomtown of Mtwara. Nasingwe came halfway.

There seemed such a sense of nothingness to the place as to take the breath away, to depress the heart. The land was flat and sandy, the sky vast and blank, the air hot and hazy. The bus stop was a single abandoned gas pump at a clearing next to the highway. A few large mango trees heavy with fruit stood languid in the sun. Beyond, a single unpaved road led into the town, of which we could see some thatched and metal roofs. Another road, more a track, diverged perpendicular to it. Civilization as I knew it, as I had just left it—the life of a city—busy streets and crowded coffee shops, baby strollers, dogs and teenagers on the sidewalks, the rumble of the subway, building cranes and digging machines—was as far away as one could imagine. It had ceased to exist. We had not seen a single other vehicle in the four hours it had taken to reach this spot. There was no airport here. No river. No newspaper. No wireless tower. And yet it beckoned, like destiny.

"Let's stop here for a night," I said.

Joseph paused, gave a quick look around. "Are you sure, Daktari?"

"Yes, I think so."

"All right," he replied indulgently.

Joseph was a young academic from Nairobi with whom I had corresponded for a few years; when I described to him my project of traversing the country of my birth by road, he had quickly proposed to accompany me, his university schedule permitting. Thus far he had been my guide and, I suppose, my protector.

He sauntered over to the driver, who was standing by his bus, and confirmed that we would be able to use our ticket the next day; we went back inside and brought out our carry-ons. The bus took to the road and departed.

The two other passengers who had alighted with us walked away. A Bajaji appeared from somewhere and idly circled around, and we boarded it just as it was about to go away empty. A Bajaji is a three-wheeler auto-rickshaw manufactured by the Bajaj company of India, though nobody here would know that. I had brought that knowledge of the world with me.

The driver was a youth called Shomari, and saying he knew of a clean guest house where we could put up, he proceeded to take us there in a reckless display of driving, as he bypassed potholes and rode mischievously into others so that we hung on to the railing behind him lest we fell off or ran into a tree. Joseph's admonishments to drive with care were of no avail. Reaching the junction he quickly swung towards the town and stopped across from a tea shop outside which a girl was standing, looking away. She wore a long blue dress with a yellow khanga draped loosely over her head.

"Halima, back in a jiffy. The bus was late. I'm carrying these gentlemen."

She turned and gave an almost imperceptible nod.

Shomari grinned happily.

"Your girlfriend?" Joseph asked.

Shomari's smile was still on and perhaps that was the reply. He did an expert U-turn, and before we could express our confusion, drove back towards the town exit, then turned left, and we were on the other road, bumping along faster than before. The young man was now in a hurry.

"What is this guest house?"

"It's a good one. My sister's. She's been to school."

Beyond the shallow green strip on our right was the silent highway; on our left was a dense growth of trees and shrubs. A steady sandstorm, churned up from the road, bit into our faces, against which we had little shelter but our hands. Just when we asked our driver how far was our destination, we had arrived at two cement gateposts. There was no gate or fence.

Shomari went through and stopped outside a whitewashed house with a veranda and sloping metal roof, an imposing presence in the wilderness.

As we got off, Shomari called out to someone inside, "Nuru!—I've brought guests!" He turned around his rickshaw and disappeared. A woman with a long face, dressed similarly to Halima, had appeared on the porch. She didn't say a word but went back inside and we followed her to a high counter, behind which she now stood. She pushed a ledger towards us.

"How many days?"

"One," Joseph replied in good humour. "After we've seen your delightful little town."

The ledger had all the usual columns plus one under the heading "Kaḅila." Tribe. I looked at my young friend, then at Nuru, and wrote simply, "Mhindi." Asian or Indian. That's what I was, as a returned native of a country I had left many years ago.

Nuru glanced at our entries, said, "Pay when you leave," and added, handing us our keys, "Numbers 2 and 3."

A long, speculative gaze followed us as we made for our rooms. I imagined her thinking, An Asian and an African, come to do what?

"She may think we are government people," Joseph said, as we simultaneously turned our keys into their padlocks. "See you in an hour? Meanwhile I'll inquire about food. I spied a chicken running about outside."

We were sitting outside on the cement floor of the veranda, next to a wooden upright. The evening was cool, and a light breeze was blowing; a rustle of leaves above and the crick-crick of insects in the distance; dark everywhere but for the white glare of the pressure lamp on the wall behind us. Before us stood the auto-rickshaw in silhouette, parked for the night by Shomari. I had gathered by now that he was actually Nuru's distant cousin. Earlier, Joseph and I had walked to the town, had tea, and strolled about aimlessly, earning not even a cursory stare—as though strangers dropped by casually every day to roam the streets. At one spot we came across Shomari's girlfriend, Halima, a tall and pretty young woman accompanied by an older woman, presumably her mother. There was no sign of the boyfriend. We saw shells of houses previously owned by Asians, who had all departed during the heyday of party socialism in the seventies. I recalled a boy in my school who probably came from one of these, and how he often returned to Dar late after the holidays due to the rains.

Idi, Nuru's actual brother, came limping over with our bottles of beer, and having delivered them retreated to sit a few feet away. He had damaged his foot in Mozambique's war of independence. I had discerned faint lines of a darker shade on his face, from which I deduced that he was a Makonde. This was a Makonde region. During my boyhood in Dar, the

Makonde could be identified by their tattoo marks, short straight lines across the cheeks and forehead; the women wore black buttons on their lips. The men were considered reliable night watchmen, and my father's shop had one called Sabini. They spoke little, because—as I would conclude later—they were not fluent in Swahili in those days. So far on this trip, however, Idi was the only one I had seen with the tattoo marks. I had not seen any woman with a button on her lip.

A short while before, I had informed Joseph of my intention to stay a few days longer in the town. He did not ask me why, for which I was grateful. He of course found nothing attractive about it, and besides he had to return to Nairobi to teach his classes at the university.

Nuru had come to sit outside and planted herself behind us next to the open door with a mug of tea.

"Why sit behind?" I asked her. "Come and sit with us."

She said nothing and did not move.

Earlier she had prepared our dinner for us, a mildly spiced chicken curry and rice; she and Idi had finished the half portion we had left for them out of courtesy. We had to pay for the whole chicken.

"How did you come to run this guest house?" Joseph asked, turning towards Idi. "Impressive structure, this," he added, casting an approving eye around.

"Our father was in government. It was an office then. When he died, we inherited it."

"So it belongs to the government."

"Nobody bothers us. We've paid our dues."

From the evidence of his game leg, he was right. He had been in the National Service, he said, and was sent to assist the freedom fighters in Mozambique across the Ruvuma, where he was caught by Portuguese gunfire. I myself had done the shorter term of national service required of high school graduates, and recalled being warned that we too could be sent to the border to fight. That might have been mere threat to uppity students, though we were taught gun routines and made to shoot at targets once before our term ended. Times were tense then, politically. The Mozambique freedom movement had its office in Dar only blocks away from where I had lived during my high school days. The South African ANC fighters had trained somewhere upcountry.

"You're leaving us tomorrow, then," Nuru said at length, her soft voice barely disturbing the silence.

Joseph was only too pleased to respond. "Me, I'm taking the bus tomorrow, but Daktari here—"

After a moment's hesitation, I said, "I'll stay a few more days. I'm not sure how many."

A look of concern came over my young friend's face. "Daktari," he said, "are you sure? You don't know about such places. You've been away too long."

"You go ahead, I'll be all right."

"I'll be waiting for you in Nairobi."

"I'm grateful."

The brother and sister were watching us.

The next day, after a morning jaunt to the town, Joseph and I headed to the bus stop in Shomari's auto, where I bade my friend goodbye. Having watched the bus disappear eastward into the glare, I walked back to the guest house. In that silence then I felt a sense of utter aloneness in the world and yet also a strange feeling of contentment. Nobody here knew who I was, where I came from. If I dropped dead suddenly they would not know what to do with me except bury me quickly according to custom. But this was what I had chosen, to step off the bus that had been my life, my sansara, as my elders would have called it. The opportunity presented itself, daring me, and I had taken it. I had a notebook and a few pens and pencils with me, which I intended to make use of, but I could not plan my forthcoming days or even hours. That afternoon I walked to town and bought a loaf of bread, two chappatis, a bunch of spinach, and half a pound of red beans. When I returned, I agreed with Nuru on a weekly rate for my board. I needed tea in the morning, I told her, and for my supper spinach or beans would do, and chicken occasionally, but I could not pay for the whole chicken if I was going to share it. She said there was no fridge, therefore if I wanted chicken I would need to buy the whole of it. I need not share it. I apologized.

—

The first several days inched past on a turtle's back; as though, in Einsteinian terms, time had dilated. I spent much of it sitting on the raised veranda, looking out, musing. How long could I survive this stillness, how would the hours and days pass? But there was no going back, there was no going back. If one day passed, the others would, surely, in a similar fashion. The trick was not to think about time as external to myself. My routine was my clock. In relativistic terms, again, my frame of reference was where I was now and what was around me.

I would notice a look of bemused surprise on Nuru's face at seeing me still around in the morning, that I had not cracked my resolve and slunk off to the station and quietly disappeared. But within a week, I estimate, I had been accepted as part of the scene and daily routine. The veranda was a good place to have my meals. Any leftovers I threw off as instructed at a dump a decent distance away, where hyenas in the night and crows in the day wreaked their quiet havoc and Idi started an occasional fire. I walked to the town every morning, where I had a cup of tea with maandazi, a sweet fried bread, and watched the local scene for a while, before returning with some produce, usually spinach, peas, or mangoes. Passersby had taken to greeting me. In the afternoon, I took another walk, in the opposite direction. I had brought two novels with me, which I read very slowly, and listened to a story or music broadcast on the old-fashioned shortwave radio which by some prescience I had purchased in Masasi. One afternoon, listening to Handel's *Samson* in my room, I gave in to a fit of crying, the tears falling in streams down my cheeks. Some inner pain, deeply harboured, was washing itself out.

One night, the three of us sitting outside in the darkness lit only by the lamp behind me, Nuru asked me about myself. I answered that I was born in Mtwara, where I went to school first and later in Dar es Salaam. I had gone to Nairobi and then abroad for university and found a job in Canada. I was married, but my wife and I now had separate interests. She nodded, a barely perceptible smile on her lips. I did not want to seem a foreigner, but she knew that I had returned after many years. Some of my ways were foreign—I ate with a spoon, and had once absently asked for a fork and knife to eat the chicken with. I wondered how much Joseph had told her about me.

My wife, Zohra, had recently taken to wearing tight hijabs, with long dresses to cover her large shape; with a renewed faith, she was now dedicated to the service of our Islamic community in Toronto. She was on its governing council. I had met her when I was a student of mechanical engineering in Nairobi, and she a modern, vivacious, and very beautiful student of architecture. To get her to go out with me, when others had failed, and moreover to the famous nightclub called the Sombrero, had been a triumph. Now the Book had called her. I had two daughters, one a lawyer who specialized in Sharia, and the other an assistant professor of art history. I had retired prematurely from my business of manufacturing plastic gewgaws; it was the only company that offered me a decent job when I entered Canada, and I took it over when the previous owner left. Like my wife, I became weary of the world around me; unlike her, I had turned into an avowed atheist. I had no interest in our community politics, or discussing medicines and stocks, or joining chat groups to bash America and bewail the woes of modern Islam. Two old friends had died, one from a heart attack and the other from cancer. Zohra had thought it a good idea when I mused to her about following up on my idea of going back to Tanzania and travelling, seeing it again and visiting places I had heard about as a child but had never actually set eyes upon. I don't think she cared where I was at the present moment. She was with God.

One afternoon as I sat outside on the veranda, the rickshaw driver's girlfriend, Halima, came walking over to me. I knew that she visited Nuru some afternoons.

"I want you to teach me," she said to me after the usual greetings.

"Teach you what?"

"English and math . . . and other things."

"Have you been to school?"

"In Mtwara."

"What happened? Why aren't you over there, studying?"

She sniffed, turning away. Money, I presumed, or her parents did not wish her to study. Nuru had advised her to see me.

I agreed to teach her and told her to come to me for a lesson whenever she visited Nuru.

"Don't let Shomari know."

"He doesn't like you to study?"

"He wants me to marry him and bear children. But I have ambitions."

It rained three straight days, but lightly, with intermittent periods of brilliant sunshine. The air was warm and earthy, the wet leaves gleamed full and merrily in the hazy light, the ripeness all around accentuated by a faint whiff of rotting garbage and smoke, and I became sick. It was malaria, which I had feared ever since arriving in the country, and immediately recognized from my childhood. I had never taken seriously ill in my adult years and felt miserable, shivering and aching in my bed, my only companion the radio. No one to comfort me or cajole me into putting a bit of food into my mouth, no one to put a cool hand on my forehead, pull the blanket over my body. I wondered if I should go to Mtwara to a hospital; but that would be admitting defeat. I had bought some weekly malaria pills in Masasi and recalled Joseph's advice to take them daily if I was struck. Aware of nightmarish side effects, nevertheless I began swallowing them. On the third day, almost starving, I asked for soup and bread. Nuru made a potato soup and Shomari was dispatched to bring bread from the town. From then on, realizing perhaps that I was only human, Nuru began bringing me my soup and stale bread. Once she checked up on me at night, saying I had been shouting in my sleep. Yes, because a fiend was roasting me in Hell for having once eaten a ham sandwich. After a week, I was over the worst, lying cool on sweat-drenched sheets that were then changed.

One night shortly thereafter she came to me in my room and sat down. She put her hand on my forehead, how good that felt, made the heart heavy with want, then told me in a tender voice to go to sleep. As I turned away, she slipped into the vacant space beside me.

The intimacy we developed remained tentative and exploratory, at times clumsy, but gradually over the days a restrained familiarity developed, a guarded mutual affection that was never articulated in words. I was still the stranger. My other involvement was with Halima; we had contacted a bookstore in the capital, and she purchased a few books that I helped her to select, sending money by phone. When they arrived, she was elated. She kept them at the guest house.

No letter came for me and my phone was dead. Any thought of that other world which I had abandoned filled me with dread. But I had to go to Mtwara to withdraw money. I returned by the same bus.

One morning I was walking to town as usual. It had been forty-three days since I stepped off the Masasi-Mtwara bus, a reminder I found somewhat disconcerting. The exact number of my days stayed current in my mind, as though tracked by an internal calendar; soon enough, I expected, and hoped, it would fade into obscurity. My thoughts at such moments usually lingered on some details of my current life, a recent incident in the clash of our different ways; she hated peas, took four teaspoons of sugar in her tea. She was casual about sex but revolted by a kiss. A kiss became a tease. My finicky personal habits, acquired in North America, I was slowly shedding; I was learning to eat with my hands again. Sitting outside on the porch at night, we told each other riddles; a recent one was: a tall old man with a golden beard and a green coat. Answer: an ear of corn. I might think of Halima: how to teach her a simple novel like *Things Fall Apart* when she hadn't the faintest notion about colonialism? That period was like a fairy story to her. I had more success with differential calculus. Recently I had advised her to read newspapers, to ask the bus drivers to bring past issues for her from Mtwara. The first batch had arrived.

And that almost proved my demise. Suddenly in the midst of my thoughts I heard the throbbing of Shomari's auto close to my ears and in an instant it had knocked me to the ground and sputtered away. The instinctive cry I had uttered faded into the landscape as he glanced back and our eyes met. A pain gripped my side. Shocked beyond words, I struggled to get up, dusted myself, spat out the sand from my mouth. I was almost halfway to town and could have turned around but defiantly hobbled onward and completed my routine. I had my tea and maandazi, bought three ears of corn and a packet of sugar, and started back towards home—as the guest house had now become for me. Shomari drove over and casually stopped to offer me a ride. My pain was so intense that I was grateful to accept. But we didn't speak.

Nuru told me, attending to my bruises, that Shomari and Halima had quarrelled. Apparently I was having too much influence on her. She had talked back at him, and he was hurt. He thought he was losing her. She had already revealed her ambition to go abroad. But he continued to bring her to the guest house in the afternoons, and each time gave me a sullen eye. Halima never asked me about the attack.

Guests arrived, three officials on their quarterly tour from the district office in Mtwara. A large white Land Cruiser could now be seen raising dust on the local roads; at night it stood like an oversized sleeping beast outside the guest house. They were a boisterous lot, dressed in what in the political seventies used to be called the Nyerere suit, a collarless short-sleeved tunic of polyester and matching pants. Their familiarity with the house and its two owners was disconcerting to me, now that I was beginning to think of it as home. One of them was called Juma, with a chubby face and satiated government employee's paunch; he wore white or beige, clean and pressed, obviously a badge of distinction. Nuru's silent blushes at some of his comments spoke much to me. On their first evening, the five of us sat for our meal out on the porch. She had fried the ocean fish they had brought, which we had with spinach and maize meal, Juma providing, in addition, Indian mango pickle in a bottle. It became apparent from the men's bluster that they were up to nothing more than checking trading licences and looking for the odd illegal Mozambican, while taking bribes where they could. After two bottles of beer each, they staggered off to their rooms. That night I asked Nuru about Juma. She did not reply and we did not speak further.

The next morning before they left for town, Juma hovered in the front office, leaning over the counter, chatting up Nuru. When he offered her a wad of notes, she refused them, saying she would give him his bill later. He turned and eyed me with a sardonic smile. "It's dollars now, is it," he said to her. The three men returned for lunch, and later when Juma attempted to grab her casually by the hips, she smacked his arm with, "Mind your manners." Huna adabu. More words were exchanged. That night after our meal, chicken and red beans with rice, he watched her come into my room and made a cutting remark about the Asian who could pay her more. Things were getting nasty.

I asked Nuru how long she had known Juma. Had she accepted money from him? For being nice to him. Came the retort, "Do you think it's easy to feed yourself here?" That blush, and the flaming eyes. I said I was sorry.

The next morning, angry words were exchanged in the reception room as I began to set off on my jaunt. Juma sounded harsh and threatening, and Nuru screamed her retorts at him in a voice I had not heard from her before. They both stopped abruptly when they saw me come out, and he pushed past me as he strode off to his room. I muttered a brief goodbye and left.

Halfway to town, at almost exactly the same dip in the road where Shomari had jostled me, I heard the metallic whine of the Land Cruiser approaching behind. I took a step further inside, slowed down, and kept walking. But the vehicle came to a dead stop, I saw two men jump out, Juma in the lead waving a machete. And I ran, shouting empty protests, hoping perhaps to be heard and rescued. Juma's curses were barely comprehensible, but they were all, it seemed to me, about my being an Indian. It occurred to me that my running only got his blood up as he panted after me and swore. I stopped then to face him and we sized each other up, his face contorted in a fury, his machete arm lowered for the moment. I said, "What have I done to you? We should talk." That was comical, and I knew it even as I said it. He raised his machete and I turned and ran. He was younger, and despite his paunch he was fast. But just then Shomari's auto came roaring down the road. We stopped and stared at it as it slowed down into free and glided towards me. Shomari stopped beside me, said, "Ingia," get in, and with me inside he turned his vehicle around and drove me back to the house. "They would have killed you," he said simply as I stepped out and thanked him. Wouldn't he rather have seen me dead?

That evening and the next day the three men came and went, speaking only among themselves, and they ate in town. I discussed with Nuru the likelihood of their reporting me to immigration authorities in Mtwara. She said it was certain that they would do so. They would return with police. Perhaps I should simply leave, I said. "If you want to," was her reply. "You know I don't want to go," I told her, and her look melted.

The following morning the men were not around, and the Land Cruiser was gone. When I asked her about them, she informed me that they had left, and I could walk to town without fear. I set off, only partly relieved, debating with myself what tomorrow might bring. The image of the attack still vivid in my mind, I could not help turning around for a quick glance behind me. The sight of Shomari's auto would have been a relief. As I approached that fateful dip in the road, I became aware of an unusual smell in the air, which I discerned as burning rubber and smoke. Farther along, the smell very strong now, I saw the terrible sight of a burnt-out vehicle spewing up thin black wisps. The Land Cruiser. It had run off the road, partly into the undergrowth. There were four men at the site, including Shomari, his auto close by. An old green Land Rover was parked some yards ahead. One of the fellows was a burly man in a torn T-shirt to whom I had given handouts of spare change a few times. I stared open-mouthed, my eyes teary from the smoke. Shomari came and told me to return to the guest house, the three charred bodies were being removed from the vehicle now. He offered me a ride back and I took it.

I reported the incident to Nuru and she replied calmly, "It was written. From Allah we come and to Him we return." We exchanged a look. "No one to hassle you now," she added.

That afternoon, after my lunch I took my walk into town. I noticed that the Land Cruiser had been overturned into the bushes and the road was clear. It even looked swept. In town, people had gathered outside the local mosque, witnessing a sheikh saying prayers over the three bodies, now wrapped in white cotton and ready to be transported to Mtwara. Shomari took me back, for it was very hot. When we passed the overturned vehicle, I asked him what might have happened to it. He said the engine probably overheated. But it was wise not to talk about it, the police would come from Mtwara to investigate. I should keep myself away then.

Halima announced shortly after that she was getting married to Shomari.

A SHOOTING IN DON MILLS

"Mrs. Lalji . . ."

"Yes?"

She recalled seeing him in the lobby when she took the elevator up. He did not seem threatening, a tall man with a soft, ruddy face and a modest paunch under his open suit jacket. Thin strands of grey hair had been combed neatly over his bald head. What did he want? Who was he? She could guess.

"May I come in, Mrs. Lalji?"

"What do you want?"

"I am from the police." He showed her his card. Kevin Leary, Inspector. Community Outreach.

She stepped back inside. "Come in."

He followed her to the living room and sat down on the upright chair next to the television. Yes, he said, he would have tea, and she brought him a cup of sweet Indian chai. He took a sip and liked it.

She stood staring at him for a moment, then went and sat down on the long sofa opposite him.

"I don't know if you heard, Mrs. Lalji . . . that Officer White—"

"I heard. He was shot and killed some days ago outside the mall. In the parking lot. I was in Vancouver then."

He was silent, then came out with, "Yes."

"You came to tell me this?"

"Yes, Mrs. Lalji. Based on the fact that in October 1976 you lodged a complaint against Officer White."

She took a deep breath. She said, "He was an animal. There was another policeman with him too that day. Granger. But that was a long time ago. And your police did nothing. Why have you come now?"

"Just a goodwill call. We are sorry we could do nothing about the incident. There were no witnesses."

Sorry his head, she thought. They are all one.

"I myself was not here at the time. I was in North Bay."

"Have they found the killers?" she asked.

"Not yet. There is one suspect. He was seen running from the scene, and we believe we know him. A young Asian-looking man named Idris—Idris Pal. He hangs around the kebab place sometimes."

He eyed her as he said this. She did not respond.

"A tall man with dreadlocks." He demonstrated with both hands. "You may have seen him at the mall."

"Yes, it's possible."

"Well. We thought we'd tell you. Officer White is dead."

"And the other one is still around."

His head jerked and he gave her a quick stare.

"I'm sorry to have brought it all back to you. We just thought you would want to know—for your closure."

You didn't bring it back, she thought. It's been with me all the time. You did nothing when you could, you stuck together. I don't know what closure is, but it is I who have closed the matter. Only half of it. And I waited a long time.

It was she who had hankered to get away to Canada. Asians were leaving Tanzania in droves during those difficult days of socialism. There were people from Dar already in Vancouver, Toronto, Calgary, sending back wonderful reports, unbelievable photos. Everything they had imagined Europe and America to be. There were good jobs to be found, people had bought cars within a few months and lived in beautiful high-rise apartments overlooking green valleys and hills. There was safety, opportunity, abundance in Canada. In Dar they had to queue up for bread early every morning and pay a bribe to get any little thing done officially. They had not seen such days before. Why not us, she told Kamru, her brother. We're no better or worse than those who've gone? The two of us will go first, and then we'll send for Ma and Bapa. He agreed, though he was reluctant at first. The parents acquiesced readily. Our lives are over, you two look after yourselves.

She was a shorthand-typist at the office of the lawyer A.K. Mawani, and word was around that they needed typists in Canada. She and Kamru both applied to immigrate. Kamru was rejected, but Gulnar was accepted. They decided she would go, and Kamru would follow, even if she had to sponsor him from there. The door had opened for them. She left for Toronto. It was the first time she had flown in an airplane. To London via Cairo, then on to Toronto in May.

Canada was wonderful and yet not always quite so wonderful. It was clean and beautiful, orderly, and abundant. The air-conditioned supermarket took your breath away every time you entered, a lit-up funfair of packed shelves and heaps of foods, some of which you had never heard of before. She put on weight despite being careful. But the faces on the streets were different, the sounds alien; the clean air blew with a certain chill; she was not used to such open spaces. And there was the humiliation of not knowing how to do or name things, of not speaking the right way, of being intimidated and called names, of just being afraid. There were nice people too, of course—who taught you how to use the bus and subway and readily gave you directions. Her first job was part-time at a Dominion supermarket in her neighbourhood, stacking supplies every Monday and Friday before opening. A big comedown from the Dar lawyer's office, though she didn't mind. She was earning money. Dollars. A few weeks later she applied for and was offered a job downtown as a typist at a legal office. She was set.

She had rented an apartment in one of the Flemingdon Park high-rises in Don Mills, where there were already other folks from back home. They seemed to be many, though actually they were perhaps fifty at most. Often, catching the elevator you would meet someone from Dar, and with relief burst out in a spate of Kutchi or Gujarati, which had been pent up unspoken inside. In the basement of the local mall the former denizens of Dar rented a room where they held their khano, their religious gathering, every weekend in the mornings at four and evenings at six. At the khano all their sense of alienation fell off. Information was exchanged, including the specials that week at the mall, new arrivals and visitors were greeted, food offerings were brought and auctioned. The steady news from Dar always reminded them of how fortunate they were to have escaped the hardships there.

Unabashedly they would recite their Arabic prayer and sing their Gujarati ginans. On festival days they would play a music tape and dance the raas. It was on these days of their muted celebrations, however, that the feelings of doubt and regret about where they were and the certainty they had lost would fall upon their gathering, for they would recall the joyous celebrations that took place in Dar, when a few thousand people sat together for the communal feast, and people danced the dandiya-raas to a live band well into the night and the music reverberated unrestrained throughout the city. On the final evening a stately procession led by the elders wearing red robes and gold turbans, accompanied by the beat of a dhol and the sound of a trumpet, would make its way through the neighbourhoods. Everyone was dressed in their finest. The khanos of Dar, prominent city landmarks with clock towers, were adorned with series of lights. All that, they had left behind. But then they had also left behind bribe-giving, food queues, ruined schools, and racial discrimination, and come to freedom and safety, even if imperfect. Gulnar prayed for her brother and her parents to be allowed to join her, so they could be a family again, even if in new circumstances. She had hopes of getting married, but not before they arrived. She wanted to learn to drive and buy a car, but she would wait.

Kamru's application was rejected again. Gulnar had half expected that, for he had no qualifications except as a shopkeeper, and so she applied to sponsor him. In her interview she showed them that she could support him when he arrived; her expenses were modest and she had a savings account. She had a letter from her employer. Besides, Kamru would be certain to find a job soon. He spoke English well, and he was a businessman; wasn't a shop a business? He did his own bookkeeping.

She was keenly observant in her faith. Back home—as she couldn't help thinking of Dar—she went to khano every evening at six, and on Friday mornings at four. Here in Flemingdon Park, she went to all the three evening gatherings of the weekend and the early-morning ones on Saturdays and Sundays. Even in the winter, in the bitter cold. In Toronto the spiritual need was greater. Four a.m., the quietest point of the night, was the designated time to meditate. The meditation brought her a sense of calm and well-being, a perspective that told her what should be important in her life, and what was merely superficial and transient. Not everyone went, of course. But those who did were a special group, a spiritual club for whom the fate of the soul was everything.

If I want to get married and have children, should I be so spiritual? she sometimes wondered. She had yet to live a life of the world. A life of the senses. She desired the presence of a man beside her, to feel a baby in her belly, a child at her breast. This made her feel guilty and blasphemous, but she said to herself, Our faith asks us to lead a life of the world too, doesn't it?

Among that first group of Dar immigrants in Flemingdon Park were a few couples with young children, a widowed grandma who was a darling, and two men and three women, all single like her. One of the men was called Amin, modest in manner and respectful, perhaps because he came from a small town, Kigoma. She had never visited it, on the shores of Lake Tanganyika and at the end of the railway line. He worked as a night security guard at the mall but went to college during the day to study accounting. He would sometimes grin and say, "This is what happens when you don't pay attention in school, even when the teachers beat the lessons into you. You become a watchman."

At a little before four in the morning on weekends he would come over from his duty and help to set up the prayer hall in the basement. Gulnar and another girl, Kulsum, would be there already. The three of them were the Set-up Committee. There was the floor to be vacuumed, prayer books to be placed at the front on a low table, the incense to be lit and taken around to every corner to render the place sacred. At exactly four the lights went out. At five a soft alarm would sound, the lights flickered on one by one, and after a recital of a ginan they would share the blessed water, niaz, in small cups. Afterwards, chatting cheerfully—you couldn't help but feel good—they would go and sit at McDonald's or Dunkin' Donuts.

They were Canadians, almost, and beginning to settle and to dream. Amin was an attractive prospect for both Kulsum and Gulnar. He became an accountant finally, but ended up marrying neither of them.

The pink face of the inspector was intent upon her, he was saying things which she did not follow. Her head felt heavy, she needed to take her nap. She got up and brought back two glasses of water. When would he leave?

"It's been a long time," she said.

"I'm glad you think of it that way, you've put it behind you."

"But I've not forgotten."

Every day all these years I've said to myself the same thing, I wish they die a horrible death, these men, White and Granger, who dirtied me indelibly; I wish and pray they meet a terrible death. But such men don't always get what they deserve.

"You know what they did," she said.

He did not respond. They never believed her then, it was her word against two of their own.

When she was young, sometimes during the holidays she joined her mother and other women of the neighbourhood on their long walk to the morning congregation. They made their way slowly up an eerily dark and depleted Uhuru Street, and could be heard blocks away, people said, the light shuffling and the soft murmurs approaching or receding. No untoward incident on the way had ever been heard of. Here in Flemingdon Park too it felt safe, even when she walked alone to the khano in the mall basement. All was as still as in Dar, except the street lamps were brighter, the buildings loomed larger. Only the cold was a worry, in the winter. A few times the men had been stopped by police cruisers, curious to know where these immigrants were headed to at this hour. Amin was one of those who were stopped, and when he explained that he was going to pray, he received a ride to his destination.

He boasted that the angels had hailed him and flown him over. One morning the cops appeared outside the hall, and having spoken to a few people as they arrived, and watched the silhouettes already sitting cross-legged in the darkened room, they departed. It was joked that the two policemen had seen the light in the dark.

Some weeks later, in early spring one morning, Gulnar came out of her apartment building and had hardly walked fifty yards on St. Dennis Drive when a police cruiser braked beside her.

"Where are you headed at this hour, Miss?"

Gulnar turned and smiled. "I'm going to pray," she replied primly.

"To the khano, we know. You should not be walking alone at this hour. And it's too cold. Hop in at the back, we'll chauffeur you there."

It was Officer White.

She didn't want to hop in, but who was going to argue with two cops, so she got into the car and they drove on and turned into Don Mills Road, then into the mall parking lot.

"Shall I get off here?" she asked.

"'Shall I?' . . . Well, well," Granger, the driver, turned around and grinned. "If you want to."

"But if you are nice," said his partner, "we'll drop you right at the entrance."

There was something in the voice, and that briefest

exchange of looks between them. Suddenly she was frightened, and froze. The two officers had opened their doors and rapidly got out and were at the back now, on either side of her. She tried to push past White, who was on her right. "I'll get off here, please let me go." But they were too powerful; one held her by her arms while the other quickly reached and pulled down her panties. They took turns with her and later even dressed her before dropping her off at the entrance. "Now, not a word to anyone," warned White edgily to her back as she stumbled away. The other one added something.

She hurried, half stumbled to the mall entrance; she hit her head against the glass door, and inside, she lurched forward and vomited, threw her guts out. She would remember her breathless cry of "Ya Ali, Ya Ali, Ya Ali, Oh God!" She barely managed to go down the basement steps to the prayer room, which was already dark, it being just past four. She ran inside for its shelter, choking on her sobs, "They . . . they . . . they . . . and fell down with a thump. No sound came in response, it was as though the room were empty, but for that faint human odour and a stirring somewhere in the air. Moments passed before a dim light came on hesitantly at the back, then more lights and they ran to her assistance.

The women took her to the washroom first. When they returned, the men had held a conference, and they all then went to Gulnar's apartment to discuss the matter further. Over a quick cup of tea they planned a strategy. It had not been her fault, she should not be afraid or ashamed. She had been attacked. And those two cops should not get away with that; they should be punished. Or they would go on and target someone else. Gulnar should file charges at the Eglinton Avenue police station. She agreed and they helped her think through her report. It was understood that the women who had washed her would testify to the rape. They were eight and all decided to accompany her.

At the station they were made to wait as though they had come in with a trivial matter. While they waited, cops came and went, drunkards and brawlers were brought in and dealt with. It was an hour before Gulnar was summoned and taken by herself to a conference room to tell her story to four grim-looking officers. They looked older than the other two. But it was clear from their cold stares that they were not going to believe her. Are you sure it was a police car that gave you the ride? How could you tell in the dark? It could have been two men dressed as officers in a police car. A cruiser, she was informed, had in fact been driven away by miscreants at about that time outside Dunkin' Donuts; the two officers would be reprimanded for losing their vehicle. They were White and Granger, whom she was accusing of having picked her up and violated her. She should not take this matter lightly. If she insisted on her accusations, she could be charged with mischief and even lose her immigration status. What were they up to anyway, men and women meeting in the dark at four in the morning—doing what? Could it have been one of her friends who was responsible, and now they had decided to blame the police? The cops were there to serve and protect, to serve and protect, she should bear that in mind. They interrogated Amin and scared him out of his wits.

"Gul, we can't win against them," he said, as he emerged from the conference room, ruffled, as though he had just faced a pack of cheetahs or something.

Her humiliation ran deep. In the days and weeks that followed, she couldn't look in the eyes of her men friends from khano, her worship companions. What must they think of her, what must they imagine? She had been dirtied. They were men after all. When she went to see the doctor in the mall, he gave her a lecture on sex and the nurse handed her a safe-sex kit, "if you must." She was afraid to open her door, and suffered nightmares in which the two cops used all kinds of means to attack or intimidate her. Scenes of the rape clung stubbornly to her mind. Now she always walked to the morning congregation along with two others, one of them sometimes Amin. A few times a police cruiser followed them all the way.

Six months later her brother Kamru arrived, and her life filled up. She cooked for two now and they went to khano together. Through a friend from Dar, Kamru got a job at a subway booth, and soon they had a car, a white Chevy Malibu. Amin married a girl from Uganda, whom he met at a new khano that had opened on a school premises on Lawrence

Avenue. Gulnar herself had received proposals over the years. She went out a few times with a man from Uganda who was a teacher; he was her best prospect, a gentle soul as observant as she was. They reached the point of discussing marriage, but then abruptly he backed off. His mother needed caring, and so on. Almost the same thing happened with another guy, who was from Tanzania. Some excuse about a sister. She knew then that the story of her rape had spread. Even the widower with a daughter, desperate to marry her at first, later changed his mind. There were two other prospects. A white guy in her building, and an Indian Guyanese she met at work, but it was she who refused to take the friendships further. Meanwhile Kamru married and bought a house in Scarborough. Gulnar didn't go to live with him. It was eight years since she had arrived in Canada and she had hardened. But she was a good aunt to Kamru's two kids and watched them grow up. She continued to stay in the same one-bedroom apartment as before, on the seventh floor of 99 St. Dennis Drive, next to Flemingdon Park Mall. And she took the 100 bus to the city as always, to get to work. She drove her own car when she needed to. Besides her savings account, she steadily put away some money in cash in a small suitcase that she kept at the back of her closet.

Thirty years had passed. Today she would be believed with her story. There would be a hue and cry in the *Star* and she would become a hero. There would be reparations. Those bastards would be in jail.

Kevin Leary was waiting for her to speak.

"Do you believe my story?" she asked.

He squirmed. "I cannot say. But my sympathies are with you. It's been a long time. Better to let it be. Do you believe in revenge?"

"Sometimes you wish you could do something, sir, when you have been hurt so much."

He was silent and looked away to stare towards her balcony. It was a bright May morning outside. He turned to her and pronounced slowly, "James White had a good family. He had three grandchildren."

"That's nice. And Granger?"

"A widower. They had no children. I believe he's not well."

He got up and moved towards the door.

"This Idris Pal," he said, turning around to face her. "He's our prime suspect in the shooting. Did you see him often?"

"Maybe a few times at the mall. I don't pay attention."

"Yes. His mother said he received a lot of money recently. He left ten thousand dollars for her in cash on the kitchen table before he disappeared."

"Could be from drugs," Gulnar said.

"Yes. Well, thank you, Mrs. Lalji—"

"Miss," Gulnar corrected him. "I did not marry."

"Excuse me. Miss. Thank you. I appreciate your time."

Yes, sometimes there's a need for revenge. And I waited a long time.

One morning outside the supermarket, as she was about to pass the young man, she stopped and came to stand before him. She knew about him because she had seen his picture in the *Don Mills Shout*. He was so startled by her presence that his mouth opened.

"You need something, Auntie?"

She said nothing.

"What?" he asked.

"I want a gun."

"You think I carry guns?" He laughed loudly, derisively.

"Where can I buy one? I'll pay well."

"You want to do someone. Who—your husband?"

"No."

"I know people who can do it for you. You ever shoot a gun? Hold one in your hand? There's people who can do it. For money. Lots of it."

"I have a lot of money."

She told him what she wanted.

MEMORIES

—Do you remember this one? Lateef jabs a finger on his tablet, and a song comes on. Thin, high, beautiful. Ancient.

Yeh zindagi usiki hai . . .

—Of course I do!

. . . jo kisika ho gaya . . .

The love song of our time. Truly she lives who lives for love, sings a plaintive, dishevelled Anarkali, escorted by two soldiers to be bricked behind a wall. No door, no window, a living burial. Named after the glorious red flower of the pomegranate, she was the maidservant who dared to return the love of a Mughal heir. The empire stood balanced on the edge of this unthinkable passion. The story is not true, she was not real, say the historians; yet she has a tomb in Lahore which people visit. Thus, love.

Nasir thinks of Zaynab. A love not returned. Or perhaps returned, but fickle—sold and bought on Wall Street forty years ago.

—How about this one! Lateef grins toothily, pressing another link on the iPad as though it were a physical button.

It's late and Nasir thinks he might have to spend the night here at Lateef's. Two bottles of wine consumed, and on to a bottomless nightcap of the Glenlivet he bought at the duty-free. Outside this Sunday night, the wind howls and whistles, rain falls in large, audible teardrops. They say Estoril has had one of the worst Aprils in memory, but it's proved a blessing to the farmers after the previous summer's drought and forest fires. Therefore the cheap *espinafre*. Spinach soups, spinach empadas.

Dum bhar jo udhar munh phere . . .

—Wah. Now there's a heart-wrencher.

O moon, look away for a breath, so I can love him, say a thousand words of love to him.

—Truly one of the most beautiful songs, Nasir says dreamily. —The old Hindi film songs just break your heart, don't they, especially over a Scotch. Acknowledged poets, even famous ones, wrote the lyrics, not like the hacks employed today. All rhythm and no emotion these days.

—Bum-swinging.

—Crotch-thrusting.

They pause to reflect. Finally Lateef says,

—I would accompany my mother to the Ladies' Show at the Odeon once a week. Zenana Show, it was called. Every

Wednesday afternoon, packed with women, all dressed up. The air thick with perfume. Even for this women's gathering, a boy often chaperoned his sister or mother. How they cried at the tragic scenes. Sobbing all around. Even when they knew it would all turn out happily. More tears at The End. They would come out from the cinema dabbing handkerchiefs to their eyes—

—As though emerging from a funeral, my dad would say, Who died today? I'm still alive! Unfortunately, my mother would murmur in reply. Not that they were unhappy. The usual banter. Even a lame or a blind husband is still a husband, was her wisdom after his death. A woman needs a husband. She missed him. He died suddenly.

Lateef peers at him, looms across the table, and again brings down the crooked forefinger upon his tablet to continue the magic. Aladdin's lamp. Nasir smiles.

Ghara aya mera paradesi . . .

My stranger comes home . . . Nargis celebrating the arrival of her lover in *Awara*, one of the great Indian films.

—My favourite actress, Lateef says of Nargis.

—I think mine too. One day in Toronto, on my way home from the airport, the limo driver turned out to be a Russian and he sang me a song from *Awara*—in Russian! *Awara hoon* . . . I'm a wanderer. Like a star in the heavens, without a family or a home, without someone to love . . .

Lateef nods, turning towards the balcony, the scattered lights and the dark sea in the distance. Absolute silence, but for the steady rain.

Who's in his mind now? His college sweetheart in London, later his wife, died fifteen years ago in an accident at four a.m. on her way to the prayer house. Every evening at seven he lights a candle to her memory on the mantlepiece in front of her photo. The son in the photo beside hers died of leukemia. A private shrine. Believes in nothing else. Gutted. Sold off everything and moved here to Portugal. Nothing left but carefully managed fun. And memories.

Lateef in another exaggerated motion stabs at a link.

Anarkali, as the final brick shuts her in, and the mortar is applied, sings: *Yeh mazar mata kaho* . . . Don't call this my tomb, it's my palace of love. A shrine.

Nasir thinks of Zaynab.

It was all books those days. They had just graduated. She gave him her copy of *Bury My Heart at Wounded Knee* to read. A detailed account of the displacement of Native Americans from their lands. For months it was on the bestseller lists. Shortly before, the place called Wounded Knee had been occupied by a group of protesters. It was the location of a massacre of Natives. Zaynab was passionate about world peace and human rights, had gone on peace marches in college, in Oxford, Ohio. A women's college. He would tease her: Oxford,

Ohio? He lent her his copy of Erikson's book *Gandhi's Truth.* He had met her in New York, where she was visiting Falu, her college mate and his friend. Falu and Nasir went back to high school days in Dar es Salaam. Zaynab came from upcountry Tanzania, from a town on Lake Victoria called Bukoba—the other end of the universe from him in Dar. The two girls had taken Falu's large bed in her studio on Twenty-Fourth Street, Nasir the sofa. Laughing, they called out to him in the dark, Poor you, feeling left out? You can come and share the bed, but no mischief! He had retorted, self-righteously: I'm not Gandhi. When he woke up, they were already awake, whispering, listening to the sentimental old film songs, crying shamelessly. Nostalgia or love? He dared not ask. I'm not Gandhi. He should have jumped in with them. An old regret, a road not taken. She'd then moved to Manhattan, two streets up from Falu, and awaited her green card.

They spoke almost daily on the phone after that. He and Zaynab. Cost him a good portion of his monthly graduate student stipend. But she was it for him, just right. Soft, dark features. Shoulder-length hair. What other girl from their background would discuss Mandela and Gandhi with passion, and Lenin and imperialism? And Truth? She had a beautiful voice.

Yeh zindagi dene waale soon . . . Giver of life, listen. I desire nothing more from your world.

Lateef's long face grins toothily at him.

—It's the first song I remember, Nasir muses. —From when I was about four. My sisters tell me I would sing it to myself when I was yay high, running around in shorts.

He thinks, What would a four-year-old see in that tragic song? Is that single song responsible for my disposition? Or the other way round? It comes to mind when Zaynab comes to mind. It was also one of the songs on the cassette she and Falu were listening to, so tearfully, that day in bed in Manhattan. The tears might as well have been for him.

—Remember this one? Lateef breaks in. He is older than Nasir, though they grew up on the same street.

Eena meena deeka! dai dama neeka!

Gibberish from India's copycat rock 'n' roll phase.

—*Aasha*! Lateef calls out, naming the film before Nasir can.

—I remember. It was my first film. My uncle Kassam, who was always broke, who failed serially at one business after another all across the country, had come into town and somehow got himself a pickup. A red Dodge, perhaps the only Dodge in town, when only a few people even owned cars. One afternoon he loaded the whole lot of us kids, his and my mother's, into the back to go see a film at the Odeon. It was *Aasha*.

—Your uncle.

—Mother's younger brother. He would dump his three kids on her and go somewhere upcountry to start a business. Nowhere he tried worked for him, but he knew how to enjoy life. And there would be some eight of us and a mother sharing our two-room flat.

Lateef smokes. Despite warnings. Despite the recent heart episode, which he refuses to call an attack. Despite the frequent coughing fits. He's lived fully . . . but there's always more to live. Nasir wonders how much grief he's stoked up behind that cheerful façade. And how much guilt deposited at the foot of that shrine on the mantelpiece. He says,

—I still remember the licence plate of my uncle's Dodge. DSK 999. Heads turned when it passed on the street. Kids would call out the number: *DSK 999!* He had to sell it, of course. And he went to open a shop in a village near the Mwadui diamond mines.

—And he didn't make a fortune, running a business close to the diamond mines? There were opportunities . . .

—He didn't know how. But he knew how to spend. Died a couple of years ago in Calgary of throat cancer.

Lateef grins.

—Missed chance.

—He also took us to my second movie—*Anari*. You remember it?

Lateef peers at the iPad screen and does a quick search; eyes light up, the crooked forefinger swoops down like a bird of prey upon the link.

—Nutan starred in it. A very different look from Nargis. Too innocent. How beautiful they were.

—They were actresses.

—Not like the Hollywood ones. These were special.

They fall silent. A break to reflect. Lateef says,

—Was your mother beautiful?

—I didn't think so then, but I saw a photo recently, taken just after her wedding. Stunning.

Lateef nods.

—We didn't realize how beautiful our mothers were. And those old photos—what quality!—they knew how to pose for them . . . classy.

—But unappreciated.

Another song.

Sab kuchh seekha hamen, na seekhi hoshiyari.

Learned everything but guile, sings a desolated Raj Kapoor in *Anari*. The honest fool, always the loser, except that he always won at the end. This was Bollywood, remember? The Scotch still has a quarter left. Should I leave now, Nasir wonders, takes a peek towards the balcony. The rain has eased, looks like, but Lateef has his finger up, there he goes jabbing at another memory.

Bachpan ki muhobat ko . . . the love of your youth, don't wrench it from your heart / if you do remember, say a prayer or two for me.

—Who was the prettiest girl you knew when you were young?

—In high school? There was a girl we called Sprite. Don't

know why. Tingled our blood, I suppose. Rozmin Ladak. She was beautiful and proud. Walked upright, aware of all those lustful eyes upon her.

—Ladak. With a wide smile, Lateef pours them more Scotch; goes into a coughing fit, puts down his cigarette and lighter beside the tablet. He goes on:

—Rozmin Ladak. Must have been her aunt, whom I have in mind. Shirin Ladak. Beautiful, outgoing. They were smart girls, the Ladak sisters and cousins. Shirin went to London, returned with some certificate or other. Secretary, maybe. She didn't have to work, of course. And there was this guy called Shilo. You knew him? Before your time. He was rich but absolutely a loafer—playboy. Expelled from his English public school, travelled all over Europe, and finally returned to Dar.

Lateef pauses, peers at his tablet. —Back in a minute. Gets up unsteadily on his feet, hobbles off to the bathroom.

Lateef returns, takes a breather. Grunts.

—You should use a walking stick.

—Yes . . . I should. Have you seen *Road to Morocco*?

—I think so. On late TV perhaps. There were a series of Road-to movies.

—I played an extra in that one.

—You're joking. Extra?—how?

Lateef holds up a hand, looks away dreamily for a moment. He turns to explain, with a smile. After classes in London one day, he was walking back to his flat in Holborn, hands in pockets, dead broke. A dark, Indian-looking chap stopped him. Do you want to act in a film?

—Yes, I said. What film? *Road to Morocco*, he said. Bing Crosby and Bob Hope. Two pounds a day, you will dress like an Arab. But bring your own costume. I took a bedsheet.

They laugh.

—That's some story. I should look for that movie.

—I was one among a crowd of Arabs. You can't see me in the film. But I'm there. But that's not all. When this fellow, Gunasingh was his name, saw my girlfriend Shamim, he offered her a role on the spot. To play the sultana's maid. The sultana was played by Dorothy Lamour. Ten pounds a day. We were rich for a few days. But in the film, Shamim speaks only one line.

—I should definitely watch that film.

Lateef leans forward, pushes on an icon.

Ae muhobbate zindabad! Long live love!

He sits back. —Did you have a childhood crush?

—Several.

—What happened?

—All of them grandmas now. Concerned about God, grandchildren, and health. How to live longer. Pressure, cholesterol, and sugar—they have those numbers at the fingertips. And their husbands'. But what about this guy Shilo you were talking about?

Lateef ponders. Puts out the cigarette.

—Shirin Ladak started going out with this Shilo. The Ladaks were a wealthy family, as you know. There was a whole gang of these rich kids having fun . . . sports cars and so on. And then.

—And then?

—Shirin got pregnant. And the old man, her father, put a gun to Shilo's head. Sort of. You'll be driven out of town. Everyone will know about you. I know people, etcetera. So they got married. Shilo and Shirin.

He pauses, continues. —And from then on, every Ladak girl, as soon as she hit sixteen, seventeen, maximum eighteen—Shirin had three sisters, and there were some cousins as well—was married off. The Ladaks were taking no chances.

Aajaa, abto aajaa, mere kismat ke kharidar . . .

Come, come now, guarantor of my fate . . .

Lateef gives Nasir a curious grin. A curious, not a mocking grin, the latter observes.

—How come you didn't marry? You must have left a love or two behind, come on! Heartaches!

—Yes.

—And? Long time ago? One special person?

—Yes. A long time ago.

Lateef looks away, thinking. Then, more seriously:

—Have you seen her since? Do you know where she is?

He thought she might have lost it, the looks, the poise, like the other grandmas. But some months ago Falu came to town.

Once petite, she's obese now, with a double chin, attributed to diabetes, for which she injects herself constantly with insulin; but as chirpy as before. Always looks him up when she comes, never speaks of the past except this one time, when he'd taken her out for a fancy lunch. Guess where I've been? San Francisco! And guilelessly shoved a photo before his eyes. Do you remember her? And Nasir replied, drily, Yes, your friend from college, isn't she? Falu smiled, nodded, Yes, it's Zaynab. There were the two of them in the photo, Falu and Zaynab, standing against a low wall decked with flowerpots. Zaynab, still with the soft features, dark and slim as he remembered her; she'd certainly retained her allure . . . at least for him. I wonder what politics she has now. Mine turned towards safety, moderation . . . It was just like old times—Falu continued, oblivious—we caught up after twenty-five years! Kids, grandkids? No, Falu said. She's divorced. But she said she did want kids, couldn't have them. Didn't want to adopt. What does she do? Teaches in a college. And he wondered: did these two recall that night in Manhattan?

To Lateef's question now, Nasir replies, —She's in San Francisco, I heard.

Lateef becomes silent. He won't prod further.

It was just after Christmas. His university had an independent study month, where he could undertake any project; his had been to go home to Dar for his brother's wedding. His flight was from New York, and he'd come to stay a couple of nights before with Falu. Zaynab said she was off to Houston to see her parents, and they agreed to meet when he returned. Are you going to tell them about me? he asked. She smiled. How naive he had been. But what did we know yet about the verities of the world? Back in New York he stayed again with Falu, who had invited a few people over that evening for a dinner party. He called Zaynab, anxious to see her, she said why not wait until dinner at Falu's. Why don't I walk over to you now? Not now, she said. Why not? You'll see. And he saw. There was with Zaynab that night, her friend Anar, and the guy: from Nairobi, UK public school, Harvard MBA, polished to a sparkle, Wall Street. As they sat around initially with their drinks, she would not meet Nasir's eye, ignored his overtures. The discussion was politics, and to the others' heated, practiced arguments the guy would eject his clipped, considered sentences. Logical, so they seemed then. You could not help but listen. They sat down for dinner, when Falu before her lamb entrée made her surprise announcement: the engagement of Zaynab to Riaz. Nasir gave a start. His face aflame, he gave her a hard look, but there was a glint in her eye that told him, Please shut up. That was his Wounded Knee. Sword through the heart. Later Falu informed him, Riaz is from her sect. You knew that? No, I didn't. How could it matter? It did.

—You win some, you lose some, Lateef says, bringing him back.

—Or lose all.

Not quite, but at the time, yes, he'd lost all. She wrote to him a few days later that she was marrying. And he replied with a pathetic You've-got-a-friend letter. She never returned his Gandhi book; he hopes she's kept it, treasures it.

Chalari sajani, ab kya soche . . . Come, darling, why think about it now.

—Shall I call a taxi? Lateef asks.

He empties the dregs into the two glasses.

—Yes, please do.

—Alvida, says Lateef at the door when the taxi announces itself.

—Alvida, Nasir replies.

Farewell, Anarkali's last words as the last brick was shoved into place and the mortar applied around it. But, the story goes, the emperor—Akbar the Great—was a fair king. Having promised the girl's mother a favour when his son was born, he now redeemed it. He had allowed an opening at the back of Anarkali's tomb, so she could escape into anonymity. And the empire was saved from the repercussions of a dangerous liaison.

Later in his apartment, Nasir looks up *Road to Morocco*. Three stars. But the year was 1942, when Lateef would have been a year or two old at most. He wonders. Memories.

AN EPIPHANY

It's mine, this music. It's gone, this life. What more could I want, in this warm, inebriated, elevated state . . . having reached a peak, all else is down. Through the glass wall, the narrow street dark and wet, the store lights dim and varied; a thin mist drifts along like a spirit. Inside here, half silhouettes in the dim light; two couples, Swedish, you can tell, and in the far corner a British couple, you can tell. Elderly. You could invent stories here, the Swedes, close yet not familiar enough, furtive escapees from humdrum lives. The British couple, familiarly quiet and huddled, let's get away from all this, be by ourselves, or we'll never do it; a second honeymoon, sort of. The young Nepali waiter flits by, smiles; knows me as a regular, a kind of Indian uncle, a mamu; comes by way of Bangalore and Malta. From a family of doctors, he says. Believable? Reminds me of times when we too, fresh from high school, would try anything, go anywhere for a future. Like when Alau and I tried

England, landed in Manchester, expecting Immigration to be lax. Bounced off, did a tour of Greece instead, cursing the British all the way, and returned home. Where's Alau now? In Pasadena, I heard. A space scientist. Even has a meteor named after him. My second glass of select red on the table, a side of olives. The music, 60s and 70s, Elvis, Sonny and Cher, Bee Gees, Beatles, Rolling Stones. Tom Jones. Herman's Hermits . . . after all these years, here they are . . . All saying, Yes, you have lived. And I echo, Yes, I have lived and loved, been fortunate—no need to boast—went abroad, won awards—was rejected, recovered wiser and nothing matters anymore because it's all passed. And I'm ready to call it quits, pick up the stumps, as they used to say after a cricket match.

The world belongs to the young, when does one start seeing that? All of a sudden, the realization dawns without warning: it's gone. It is their world now, just as it was ours once, not so long ago, yesterday, when we walked out with such confidence, con brio, and every adult said, The future is yours, go and grab it, and we went out and it was in our hands. And it slipped through, as it must. Always. And we stepped onto the other side and here I am, when everything sounds trivial, passé, I've-seen-or-heard-it-before, and therefore, obviously, I don't belong anymore.

I predict movie endings. Plots I can place into a handful of categories. I imagine the young graduates employed to write them, new geniuses discovering the wheel, but it's your problem, I remind myself, stop railing at them, they write for their age. They can't know you. Weren't you young and fresh once? Precisely. The only difference between then and now is that the villains are different. Substitute Muslims for Germans. Novels too sound tired, contrive profundity, struggle lugubriously with metaphors, perform verbal gymnastics saying nothing. How to while away those sleepless hours, then? It's back to the classics. Your time, your books, your films, your music.

They get up for you on the subway these days, and the ladies open doors for you. Thank you, but I should have been the one to do it. The red face of old age. And do you call them ladies anymore? I don't know even that. And I don't care.

I've written what looked important once, had not been said before, so I thought loftily, but it seems laughably trite now in this turbulent world where news breaks every minute and opinion tweets at you from all directions. Moving with the times, as I can no longer do, my sober dailies sound hip now. They test your uptake like schoolmarms, give you a takeaway every morning like your school lunch. Interpret the world for you, but no thank you, we were taught to think for ourselves. That can be risky today.

The news is depressing, anyway. Hasn't it always been? The Climate. The Wars. The rich and the poor. The immigrants and the refugees. But I've done my marching, don't want to change the world anymore, let the young change it. It's their moment, not mine. Look what kind of world you're leaving for us, they mouth from their coddled homes; well, we paid the price for the luxury you have to say that. If you fear the climate, we feared the bomb . . . doomsday for us too lurked around the corner.

India was the great revelation when life was yet to be lived and expanded. It mattered, the spiritual home, the ancestral home, brought a smile to the lips. The first step I took there, I remember too vividly. That thrill too is gone. As it must. The friends I made are older or dead, the children I played with are gone abroad, everyone's connected and wirelessly chatting. And hatred has leaked into the air. No longer the Phantom India, the mystical India of pirs and gurus, of Gandhi and Truth, and Shankar and Ray. Poetry and song. The wonder that was.

To repeat, I've lived and loved, had my small successes and failures. And now the body sends its signals, eyes, heart, blood, thankfully not ears yet, but that's coming they tell you, and dementia awaits. Life is lived no longer for some lofty aim but to prolong itself, keep the numbers low and the momentum wearily rolling, cheat death. But why not invite it, laughing, or at least smiling the Buddha smile? That's truly beating death. Stop pushing and let the stone roll down—Camus—and save on resources to leave for the complaining coddled ones when they grow old. We leave you a world without us, thank us, we will not be there to torment your budgets.

No one is missed, really. The kids have their own lives, the wife will join other wives and venture out on cruises and reunions. Find a new partner perhaps. Here I am, alone, in a beautiful town by the sea, watching young life passing by, not envious—I've lived, I said—go on, young people, to wherever you're going, though you'll wind up here in the end, watching other young people walk by . . . two men in Muslim garb, Moroccans, perhaps, a couple in jeans with arms around each other, his hand in her back pocket, we know where he's headed—it's rained lightly and the mist hangs and wafts along in the spring air and the light from the coloured shop signs is reflected in the wet pavement, and the young Bangladeshi shopkeepers close their shutters and insert their padlocks, and look around wondering what to do next—it's all beautiful and quiet and I'm all alone and contented and suitably high on a good red, and no one will know if I go back to my room on the hill and overdose or something. Why not order first the fried potatoes I've been denying myself to stay healthy and then go and find my peace?

AN AMERICAN FAMILY

He reads, in the *Amherst Echo*:

> Wallace Brand, 63, died May 13 at Amherst Charity Hospital after a long illness. He was born in Baltimore, the son of Wallace T. and Marie (Livermore) Brand. "Wally" was a state trooper for seven years before attending UMass Law School. Following graduation he was legal consultant to a number of corporations and the Amherst School Board. Surviving is his wife, Laura; four children, Marie of Burlington, Vermont, Lucy of New York, Katy of Washington DC, and Tom of Provo, Utah; grandchildren Thaddeus, Lee, Ali, Sara, Paul, James, and Refat; and brother Tim Brand of Germany . . .
>
> Private interment will be at Mount Hope Cemetery, Amherst.

Two years ago, on another listless afternoon, surfing the web he'd come upon the death announcement of the older Wallace Brand, who passed away in Baltimore, aged eighty-six. And now, Wally Junior, still in middle age; cancer? Timmy's in Germany, not surprising, probably still plays with a band. And dear Marie, gone long ago. He sees them together in his mind as he saw them then, some decades ago: a small happy family in the suburbs that became his American family. That picture faded with the years, acquired context, became just one among the many from his life's journey; still, it retains that something that spurs a shot of gratitude in him whenever he sets his mind upon it.

He had said he would come by Greyhound (what else) to New York, expecting to be met at a bus station not too different from Boston's, where he had landed the previous night. In the morning he'd gone to the university to confirm his acceptance of its offer of admission, which had been put in doubt by the interference of his government. The foreign student office had been friendly, told him not to worry, plied him with literature, and offered him a coffee and doughnut; he had used their phone to call his host family in New Jersey, the Brands, who had been assigned to him by the Welcome to America Agency. In his excitement about going to America, he had rashly accepted their offer of a short stay with an American family before beginning his studies. As the bus arrived in New York, he did not feel so certain about the prospect anymore, though

Mrs. Brand had charmed him over the phone. "We're looking forward to having you," she said.

The bus entered a dimly lit tunnel and stopped at a parking bay inside a vast underground garage, buses arriving, departing, parking. He picked up his suitcase and shoulder bag and followed the other passengers out and through a modest side door up an escalator. Yes, you go up to go out, someone confirmed to him. How, in this tumult—broke the thought in his mind as he stepped off the trundling wooden steps with his bags into an endlessly large bright hall, a madhouse of people rushing hither and thither like ants in an ant-heap, when a man stepped up abruptly in front of him. "Mr. Adatia?" Mr. Brand, as he would always call him, even though he himself would soon become plain Hussein, was a round-faced, pale-faced, medium-height man in a light grey suit, looking rather frazzled. He didn't wait for an answer. "Am I glad I found you! Wallace Brand." They shook hands. "I'm here to pick you up, as promised. Let's get out of here."

It became family folklore at the Brands' how Wallace Senior, with only a passport-size photo in his hand, anxious about how he would recognize their guest among the teeming crowds at the Port Authority, had stationed himself at just the spot, the head of the escalator from the bus gates, scrutinizing every young man who floated up. "It must have been obvious," Wally Junior would say with a grin; and Timmy, "Come on, Dad, stop exaggerating." And Marie, as Mrs. Brand soon became, would remind them that their guest had been in the country less than twenty-four hours.

He can't recall the walk to the car, a big black Pontiac Grand Prix, most likely parked outside the terminal at a nearby lot, but soon they were on the hectic New Jersey Turnpike at rush hour headed for Upper Montclair, and thus began Hussein's American education, Mr. Brand chatting all the way. Why do you have to pay money to use the road?—Hussein's first question. Suppose you don't?—his second. The cops would come chasing after you on their motorbikes. See them parked at the sides? He didn't, and it was already too late. Cheerfully bright, barely comprehensible giant billboards passed by them, and green road signs, as they rode with varying speed immersed in a sea of vehicles, his eyes glued to the window. I can't believe I'm here.

They took an exit, drove into a quiet and luxurious suburban avenue, arrived in the driveway of a large, grey-brick mansion. The family were waiting for him at the door. Mrs. Brand—Marie, a big blonde with a wide, welcoming smile, Wallace Junior, stocky like his father, wearing eyeglasses, and Timmy, lanky with shoulder-length hair. Both boys with curious smiles, twinkling eyes. And Mr. Brand regaled them with his tale of the miracle meeting at the Port Authority. Dinner was waiting. Chicken, he remembers, though not how it was cooked, and Marie gaily advised him he could use his hands to eat it as the boys were doing. Yes, he would have a Coke, and a can was brought for him. You press that tab to open it, Timmy explained, and showed him how. Back home a Coke was brought only for a special guest, purchased from the corner store, and after a glass had been poured out and served, the kids would fight over the remainder. He felt intensely shy and answered haltingly their questions about his home, his city, his country. Dessert fittingly was apple pie, after which they took their plates to the sink and dishwasher, and he was shown his room in the attic, Timmy helping him with his luggage. It had a double bed, a carpet, beautiful floral curtains, and an adjoining bathroom. There was no connection, he mused when they'd left him—with instructions to come down and raid the fridge whenever he got hungry—between where he came from and where he now was, except that the life he'd left behind still existed somehow in the circuitry of his brain. He walked around the room, looked out the window at the empty street and the treetops and the sloping rooftops that could be from a storybook, then he washed and sat down for a moment on the high, soft bed. Pulling up his legs, he crossed them and silently said his prayer before laying his head down on the pillow that smelled ever so sweet. I must never forget home.

Mr. Brand worked on Wall Street at a company called Bear Stearns and left early each morning for the train station. Timmy, with the long hair and scrappy, embroidered jeans, would amble down late in the morning, strum a few strains on his guitar for his mother, and go out to be with friends. He and his brother attended a military academy in Baltimore, though Timmy had declared his intention to drop out. Wally Junior, with neat haircut and tucked-in shirts, had a girlfriend in town and had become a Mormon. The family were Episcopalian. When Hussein was not accompanying Marie in the Grand Prix as she did her chores and showed him off and around, he would read in the den and watch TV. Back in Dar there was no television; now in the rec room in Upper Montclair he consumed TV shows with the uncontrolled appetite of a starved child. *Lucy, Gilligan's Island, Hogan's Heroes, Bonanza, Gomer Pyle, Get Smart, I Dream of Jeannie, Perry Mason.* Dick Van Dyke, Flip Wilson, Johnny Carson. *Face the Nation. Meet the Press.* He learned the lingo, became aware of issues, expanded his sense of humour. He would be chuckling away over daytime reruns when Marie would call him to have lunch or coffee with her in the kitchen, where she would sometimes watch her shows. In the evening, when Mr. Brand returned, Hussein would accompany him to the local park where they jogged side by side. They had taken him into their life without fuss, an ignorant, oddly dressed, and often clumsy brown stranger.

Marie and Mr. Brand talked easily with him. Mr. Brand had joined the war in its last year and spent it in England. He didn't fight, for he'd been assigned for office work. Hussein knew about the war and D-Day from the movies. One day while searching for a sweatshirt for Hussein to wear, Mr. Brand pulled out an old shoebox from a shelf in the downstairs closet. Marie was not around. Mr. Brand fished out a snapshot from the box. It showed him in army uniform standing next to a woman. A plain-looking, thin Englishwoman in a loose dress, almost his height, with short curly hair and a rather nice squinting smile. She didn't want to come to America, she had parents, Mr. Brand explained with a nod. Back in America he had worked briefly in army intelligence, where his job was to sift through newspapers. After his discharge he attended Johns Hopkins. No, he never made it back to England. And they didn't write, he and Clarissa, no point. Marie was from Florida. She was on a bus trip to Washington DC with her three sisters when she met Wallace Brand, and they got married.

He didn't stand a chance, Marie said. Four sisters from the South had descended on the capital after the war one July, and marked him out in a hotel bar where he was sitting alone, his friends having left the table or something. Marie hit the jackpot. It was the Fourth of July. Marie was a talker, a carefree, happy personality. Often in their conversations she would mention the General, someone who had had a large influence on her life. He was, apparently, much older and had died a few years ago; Hussein gathered somehow that they had had an affair. The General had approved of Wallace Brand and helped the couple in their early years of marriage. Marie had a sister, Jane, who lived nearby, married to a tall, cheerful man, Harry Smith, who also worked on Wall Street. Always ready with a wisecrack, he made Hussein laugh. The Smiths had a daughter called Lucy-Ann, a slim girl with a ponytail and a thin, musical voice and fussy hands who had just finished her freshman year in Florida. On a Saturday before a barbecue at the Smiths' house, Hussein went to see the film *Love Story* at the local theatre with Lucy-Ann and the two boys. The book was all the rage then, and Marie had given him her copy to read, saying he would relate to it, since he was joining university himself, and he had finished it in a sitting. He enjoyed the story, though he understood Lucy-Ann when she said that university was not as it was depicted in the movie at all. At the barbecue, he had played charades with the three cousins, though he barely understood the clues or the answers.

He thinks of the Black cleaning woman who came twice a week, wonders what she might have thought of him, who came from Africa. Marie called her Jemmie, and the two chatted for long periods when they sat down for coffee in the kitchen; once Jemmie brought her son, who was perhaps in his thirties, to thank Marie for a gift of clothes. He did not speak much but Hussein shook hands with him. Did Jemmie have another name? he wonders. She did his room and laundry, but they barely exchanged more than a formality each time, and what seemed a longish look. He had an impression that she had formed a definite opinion about him. Once during their rounds in the Grand Prix, Marie stopped at a deli, where they had lunch. She suggested he order a sandwich, and when it came he gaped at the whole two inches of its thickness and then up at her. How to pick it up. She smiled. "We don't always eat like this. You'll need both hands." She herself had soup. It was a stroke of genius when he cut the sandwich into quarters and offered her a piece. When he offered to pay, as per the Welcome Agency guidelines, she put her hand over his and smiled. Two women in tennis outfits came by just then and he was introduced. They asked him about lions where he came from and he replied that you could find them in national parks. Later Marie showed him the local college, where the art instructor was very popular with the women, including those two who had come by at their table.

During his second weekend Mr. Brand drove him to Washington DC via Baltimore and Annapolis, and he saw the White House, the Lincoln and Jefferson Memorials, the Washington Monument and, what he was the most eager to see, Arlington National Cemetery and President Kennedy's grave with its eternal flame; he sensed that the Brands were not very fond of the Kennedys. He for his part had gazed in admiration at the glorious photos of President Kennedy and his beautiful wife in the newspapers back home; the US Mail postage stamp on the envelope that brought him news of his admission and scholarship had carried an image of the eternal flame. He's not forgotten the date of the assassination, to this day; he was walking home on Uhuru Street one afternoon when he saw the stark, bold *Daily Nation* headline in the hands of a vendor: Kennedy Shot Dead. Across the street from the White House now, where they had come out to stand beside the car and watch, Mr. Brand related to him how the national anthem happened to be composed, by one Francis Scott Key, and at Hussein's naive insistence, rather bravely—as he now admits—his host sang it for him. On the way back, he met Mr. Brand's mother at her apartment in Baltimore; he recalls vaguely a small, rather reserved woman with curly white hair who had brought them tea in a tray. Later, with Marie in town, they went for a seafood dinner and Hussein was introduced to lobster, clams, crab cakes; but he still refused alcohol. Marie's older sister Liz was also present, a smoking, gritty-voiced professional golf player, who drank a lot and gave Hussein a kiss on the mouth and invited him to visit her in Florida.

On their drive back, Mr. Brand cautioned Hussein not to take Liz too seriously; she had a tendency to invite young men to stay with her; the last one was called Saeed. Early the following Tuesday Mr. Brand took him to Newark airport and put him on a shuttle to Boston, insisting that that was the only way to go for his first day at university.

His introduction to America; it should have ended then, according to the Welcome Agency, but Marie wrote to him, on beautiful letter paper, and he to her, on his yellow notepad, and sometimes he called them collect. They invited him to come over for Christmas, and whenever he wished, and he became in some sense a part of their family.

Christmas Eve, he took a ride to New Jersey with a girl called Gudrun, who looked rumpled like she'd just woken up and argued all the way with her Indian boyfriend, who sat in the front beside her. With Hussein at the back were two other guys. It had snowed but was clear and bright now, and bitterly cold; the Volvo was ancient and leaky but thankfully the floor at their feet was lined with a doubled-up blanket. The white fields and tree skeletons they passed were mysteriously beautiful, silent creatures from another galaxy. Nothing like he'd seen before, though years later they would remind him of Tolkien's Ents. The three of them at the back sat jammed together in their winter jackets, and the radio played "A Horse with No Name," by a group called America, continuously, on station after AM station as they progressed. The words intrigued him though he did not understand them. The others apparently did, for they discussed it. Gudrun dropped his two fellow passengers off at a town outside New York, and him at Newark airport, where Marie picked him up.

At the house, the next morning, Christmas Day, as he sat with the family on the carpet before a tall glittering Christmas tree in the formal living room, which was rarely used, they regaled him with gifts. He recalls a Shetland wool sweater he would keep almost forever, even when it had grown holes; a portable radio; a silver ballpoint pen, a tape of gospel music, and small personal items including deodorant and a dandruff shampoo; he hadn't known what dandruff was. He gave a book about Eisenhower to Mr. Brand and a traditional Tanzanian khanga cloth to Marie; for Timmy he had brought a Johnny Cash LP, and for Wally a book on Buddhism. That holiday he visited New York City with Wally, Timmy, and Lucy-Ann, and they went up to the top of the Empire State Building and walked along Fifth Avenue to look at the decorations. He didn't care much for the city, it took him years later to get hooked by it.

One evening, they had just returned from an Italian dinner, Marie a little drunk on Chianti. He was on his way up to his attic room when, hearing an exclamation and a chortle behind him, he turned around and to his astonishment saw Mr. Brand supporting a very bald-headed Marie, holding in her hand a blonde wig. "Isn't this better, Hussein, am I not beautiful like this?" She made a clownish, grotesque face at him, to which he said "Yes" and grinned and Mr. Brand nodded to him. He went to bed shattered, in tears. It felt like someone had given him a resounding slap on the face, leaving a persistent, buzzing echo in his head so he could not even think. But when he came down the next morning, a very normal-looking Marie was sitting at the kitchen table, the local paper in front of her. She offered him a coffee and corn flakes and apologized to him for her display. She had cancer, she explained, and the chemotherapy had removed her hair. Also made her flighty, for which he should excuse her. But she was recovering, she assured him, and yes, her hair would grow back. It wouldn't be blonde, she laughed, and he laughed with her, saying he quite preferred the blonde. That Sunday he went to church with the couple, as he had done last August. He had gone out of curiosity then, and enjoyed the experience, especially the choir, but this time he also wanted to pray for Marie at her church.

Gudrun came to pick him up at the house, with the boyfriend, whose name was Alok, and Hussein guessed they had come all the way to Montclair simply to pass judgement on where in the bourgeois homeland he had put up. They were impressed by the neighbourhood but contemptuous of the wealthy Republican suburb that it was. A *Nixon for President* sticker had appeared on the back window of the Grand Prix. Hussein, like almost everyone on his campus, leaned towards the Democratic candidate McGovern; as did Timmy, but not Wally Junior.

He visited again in June. This time his ride, a French graduate student, dropped him off in Spanish Harlem, where he was unnerved to find that hardly anyone understood him when he asked for directions; he made his way to the Port Authority terminal by bus, not certain about going underground to use the subway, as directed by someone in halting English. By this time his hair was long and he had joined peaceful demonstrations against the war in Vietnam. The Brands were unfazed. The war would soon be over, said Mr. Brand. The boys were not around; Wally would be joining a college in Vermont, and Timmy would transfer to the local high school. Marie looked a little subdued and came down late in the mornings, and he worried. When he asked her if she was feeling all right, she said yes and smiled her gratitude and gave him a tight hug. Back in Boston later that summer he watched the Democratic Party convention on campus, staying up the night. In August he again visited Upper Montclair. This time he made good on a boast and cooked ground beef curry for the family that they ate outside in the back of the house; he thought it was a failure, and Mr. Smith dubbed it the gut-rumbler, but Marie assured him that it was good.

In November, soon after the presidential election, in which Richard Nixon took all the states except Massachusetts—an outcome hard to forget—Mr. Brand called him to say that Marie had passed away. The death had been painless and she had been her usual self, cheerful till the end. The family was with her, and according to her wishes she had been cremated after a small, private ceremony. He was crushed. A precious part of his new life had fallen away, and he wished he could have been at her side in her last moments.

He spent Christmas on campus, with all those who had nowhere to go, including three Ethiopians, a Greek, and a Cameroonian. Later that summer he received a letter from Mr. Brand, in reply to his, informing him that he had remarried. His new wife's name was Marilyn and he had moved into her house in Montclair proper, where she lived with her four kids. Hussein was welcome to visit them, he would always be a part of the Brand family. He visited in October. The leaves had turned, and it was wet. The new home was large and chaotic; the youngest of the four kids was a girl of six, who took a liking to him but asked a lot of questions, and there was an irrepressible little dog. The three older kids were in and out and loud. Two boys and a girl, Hussein had been given one of the boys' rooms. The Grand Prix was gone, in its place was a rather messy Buick. Mr. Brand told him that Marilyn was a client, and he had met her in church. It had been Marie's wish that he remarry. It was apparent that the relationship was still raw, Mr. Brand was trying too hard. He no longer went jogging and it was hard to get a private moment with him. Marilyn always looked harried. Hussein realized that he was simply in the way. The Smiths had left town.

Mr. Brand, assuring him that he was welcome to visit him any time, dropped him off in Eastside New York, where lived a new acquaintance of his whom he'd met in Boston earlier in the year. There was now a small community of young Asians from back home who had come to New York as tourists and stayed on to get their green cards. This was a new phase in Hussein's life and he was beginning to enjoy visiting the city.

It was two years later when Hussein found the will to call up Mr. Brand. The thought had played on his mind all along, but he had balked. While Mr. Brand had invited him to visit any time, Marilyn had pointedly not reiterated. And who could blame her. But he was now in graduate school in Philadelphia and Montclair was not far. He could easily make a day trip there. Mr. Brand would have settled into his new life now, and Marilyn might be calmer and even welcoming this time.

It was eight in the evening when he called; Marilyn picked up the phone. He identified himself as Hussein, the foreign student from East Africa who had come to visit from Boston; how were she and the kids? And Mr. Brand? There followed a moment of silence on the line, before she replied sharply, "We're fine. What do you want?" And then, before he could say another word: "Mr. Brand is not here. Your friend lost all my money and has gone back to Baltimore!" She slammed down the phone.

And now, decades later, the death notices on the internet. That picture of the happy, generous family of Upper Montclair has not tarnished, just faded. His world is more complex now. He's lived in Canada for many years and his daughter is at a law firm in New York, not far from the offices of Bear Stearns, which eventually went bankrupt. It might not be the cool Canadian thing to say, he muses, but America still has a heart in it somewhere. He had found it. Every Christmas he sends a small check to the university that opened the world to him.

ACKNOWLEDGEMENTS

My thanks to my editor Martha Kanya Forstner for her comments and observations and saving me from a howler concerning Malcolm X, and Melanie Little for her sensitive copy-editing, as before. And Nurjehan, for always being there, and Mwalimu Justus Makokha for his company during an exciting bus journey we both remember fondly. And finally, Firoz Manji, raconteur par excellence, for his generosity.